I THINK I'M ALONE NOW

ALI SEAY

Grindhouse Press
PO BOX 540
Yellow Springs, Ohio 45387

Grindhouse Press #102
ISBN-13: 978-1-957504-17-9

This book is dedicated to the 80s and to the real Mr. Frank who carried me home one day when I tripped on my own clogs and fell into the street. We were all terrified of him. I don't think he deserved it.

PART I

PART I

CHAPTER 1

1985

"OH SHIT," MELISSA SAID.

I stared. Had I really just done that? Had I really just kicked our ball over the fence into that yard next door?

"He's home," Debbie hissed. "He's home! He's home!"

She just kept saying it. The world's worst parrot.

"I heard you the first time," I groaned.

She nudged me hard with her bony elbow and I smacked her. "What are you going to do?"

"I guess I'm going to get our damn ball."

At fourteen, you'd think Mr. Frank would hold less sway over me. You'd be wrong.

He'd been the mean man in the neighborhood my whole life. The one every kid on the block avoided. The summer before he'd had an entire trashcan full of balls because most kids would rather abandon them than risk going into his yard.

"You know he eats little kids," Melissa said.

She was shooting for sarcasm, but her tone said she believed it more than she wanted to.

"I highly doubt that," I said, eyeing up the simple chain link fence.

I THINK I'M ALONE NOW

I wasn't the graceful sort. I liked to kick a soccer ball around like everybody else, but "athletically inclined" were not words anyone in their right mind would use to describe me. That being said, my brother Eric had given me that stupid ball for Christmas and I happened to like it. Mostly because Eric was six years older and had picked it out himself. He was a good big brother and I missed him now that he'd moved out. It meant more time with Frick and Frack.

"He might be a perv," Melissa said. Her big brown eyes were even wider with anxiety.

"He might be. Most people are," I said over my shoulder as I braced my hands on the fence. "But I doubt he's going to chase me around naked waving a rubber chicken."

"Eew," Debbie said.

That made me laugh and I nearly face planted into Mr. Frank's yard. Instead, I broke my fall with my hands, bending my wrist back harder than I'd have liked. I muffled my own cry, suddenly aware I had fallen into enemy territory, and I didn't want to be detected.

"Are you okay?" Melissa asked, peering through the chain link.

I sat up, brushed dead leaves out of my hair, and spit out a few blades of grass. "Totally fine."

"Good going, Grace," Debbie said.

"You want to get the ball?" I asked.

She backed up a step, shrugged, and mumbled, "It's not my ball anyway."

I stood up, pissed off from the scare the fall had given me. I had scratches on my palms and dirt in my hair. "Whatever," I snarled.

I risked a glance at the back door to Mr. Frank's. Like every other house in the neighborhood, it had been built in the late sixties and now, in the mid-eighties, was considered highly outdated. But also like every other house in the neighborhood, it was well taken care of. We took pride in our houses around here. Mr. Frank more than most.

"He hasn't raked his leaves yet," I muttered. "Surprising."

"Surprising he's not out here picking them up with tweezers," Melissa said. Then she snorted, having amused herself.

"My mother said it was because he read an article about letting the leaves compost being better for the garden in the spring," Debbie piped up.

I grunted, not impressed.

"But then my dad said he was getting old and lazy."

At fifty-something Mr. Frank was old to us. He was ancient. When you're fourteen, anyone over the age of twenty is on the verge of dying.

I finally found the bright green and orange ball back by his fig tree. It had rolled beneath it into a patch of shade that virtually swallowed it up.

I squatted down to get it, both my knees popping so loud it sounded like sticks breaking.

Both Melissa and Debbie fake gagged in the background. I giggled. They did that every time my knees cracked, and it always made me laugh. For some reason, the noise bothered them.

I was backing out on all fours, wondering how I was going to explain the dirt all over the knees of my jeans to my mom, when I heard the back door creak open.

I assured myself it was probably my imagination. I was probably wrong. But the fact that Debbie and Melissa both shut up instantly told me I was not imagining it. He'd opened his kitchen door.

"Doris, is that you?" he called.

The hair on the back of my neck stood up when I realized he knew my name. I had lived across the street from him since I was born. Why this was surprising to me, I have no idea.

But, no. It wasn't so much surprising as disturbing.

If you were a kid, the last place you wanted to be was on Mr. Frank's radar.

I took a deep breath and braced myself to run. If I had to, I would. I'd run right out his back gate and into the alley and around the neighborhood if I had to. If it meant not getting in trouble with the dreaded Mr. Frank.

Rumor had it he'd once beat a neighbor kid with his belt for dropping a tennis ball in his garden.

Here, I'd just crawled through the same ground. I had the filthy jeans to prove it.

"It is," I said.

I got hot then. A sudden flare of heat. A brushfire under my skin. Mr. Frank seemed to twitch. Recoil slightly. But it was just the shadow of the fall leaves shifting on the branches.

"Sorry, sorry," I said. I was trying to gauge which direction to go.

He took a step toward me, studying me.

I could feel Debbie and Melissa holding their breath. Terrified.

My heart pounded, and my toes itched. Ready to run. I wasn't athletic or fast, but I was a tomboy and I would totally run full tilt even if it meant falling on my face.

"Did you get it?" he said, throwing me off guard.

"Huh?"

"Your ball. Did you get it?"

I pulled it out from behind my back as if that had in any way been shielding it from his eagle eye.

"Yep. Sorry again. Mr. . . . Frank. Sorry." I sounded like a broken record.

"Can I speak to you a moment, Doris?"

Fear, hot, sudden, and overwhelming, coursed through me.

He flinched again as if he could read my mind. Or maybe he was realizing the creep factor. Mr. Frank dressed in his nice slacks and button-down short-sleeved shirts with his white undershirt peeking out at the neck even if he didn't have anywhere to go. He did yard work in dark green mechanic coveralls the same color as my grandfather's push mower.

If this were a movie, he'd be the guy. The killer. The villain.

"I'm not supposed to—"

"Come now, I'm not a stranger. I'm your neighbor. Since you were a baby."

My nose twitched like a hunted rabbit. My feet tingled to run. And then Dandy, Debbie's dog, came busting out of her screen door, making it slap loud against the frame. He stood there breathing hard, slobbering the way St. Bernards do, and then he sneezed mightily, sending a ribbon of drool flying onto Melissa's arm.

The spell was broken when Mel shrieked in disgust and flung her arm back, thus flicking the drool ribbon onto Debbie who promptly squawked in distress.

My legs moved, I smiled a fake smile and said, "Sorry again, Mr. Frank. Won't happen anymore."

Then I made a beeline for the back gate which seemed to flip open in anticipation of me touching it. I was moving so fast and was so eager to leave, it all jumbled together.

I jogged down the street, took a right at the bottom of the hill, took another right at the bottom of the next street and ran full out up my street and to my front door.

My mother ripped open the door when she heard me fumbling with the knob.

"Dorrie, I was just about to call for you. It's dinner ti—" Her gaze had found my fouled jeans and she frowned.

They were new pants for school because I'd had a growth spurt. They were about a week old and I wasn't supposed to wear them to hang out with my friends.

"Sorry," I said. "I fell." I was hoping for some sympathy.

It didn't work.

"You shouldn't have had them on either way." She stepped back to let me in. "Go put some stain remover on them. Pronto!"

I hurried to do as she asked, but at the last moment, I glanced across the street.

Mr. Frank was watching me from his front window.

I pushed past my mother into the safety of my house.

CHAPTER 2

THAT WAS HOW IT STARTED with Mr. Frank. Instead of telling my mom, something we'd totally do nowadays, I kept it to myself. I wanted to know why he wanted to talk to me. I wanted to know why he'd been watching me. People threw the word perv around a lot. But I didn't think that's what Mr. Frank was. Weird, yes. Intense, you betcha. A perv? No.

Mrs. Frank—I mean, I had no idea what their last name was mind you—had died a few years before. I think her name was Clara, but I wasn't sure.

Ever since her death, he'd doubled down on yardwork. Housework was a big thing, too. Washing his car. He crammed the time once filled with a spouse with tidiness and neatness. And watching us kids with an eagle eye.

Me, especially, apparently.

My mother knocked once and stuck her head in, "Mellie is on the phone." Then she smiled. It seemed I was forgiven for my fucked up jeans.

"Thanks. I'm coming."

My mother insisted on calling Melissa "Mellie" even though she hadn't gone by that since we were seven.

I grabbed the phone receiver and the base and dragged it back to my room. I wasn't allowed to have a phone in my room, but my mother had put the hallway phone on a ten-foot cord so I could take it in my room when using it. What the difference was, I had no idea.

"Hey, Mellie," I said in my most syrupy voice.

"Honestly, she won't stop," Melissa said.

I shrugged and flopped back into my nest of pillows. "Yeah, but don't worry, she still calls me Doris a lot. So, there's that."

"Mothers."

"Yes, mothers."

"You okay? You took off outta there and then my mother called me in for dinner and Debbie had to go in and, you know, I'm still covered in dog snot."

"It's drool," I said.

"Whatever. It's gross."

"So, get in the shower, stupid."

"I will. I wanted to call you first. What do you think he wanted?"

"Who?" I played dumb, but I don't know why. My face was hot again. Sometimes, I got warm and my skin felt about two sizes too small. My mother said it was hormones, but sometimes I worried I was going to be like an episode of *Unsolved Mysteries*. I was going to self-combust and no one would know why. I could picture the smoke on the screen and hear the host's haunting voice.

"Who do you think? Mr. Frank!"

I smiled. I liked making Melissa squeak like that. It meant she was frustrated with me.

I'm evil.

"I don't know. He's very strange. I think he might be lonely."

I wasn't sure if I actually thought that, but it seemed to make sense.

"Do you think he's . . . after you?"

"After me? What's this? An after-school special? You watch too much TV, Mel."

"It was just weird. You're fourteen and he's like a hundred."

"I think he's in his late fifties."

"Close enough."

"I don't know. I guess we'll see if he bothers me anymore. I doubt it."

"Did you tell your mom?"

For some reason that put my back up. "No! And neither will you."

"But—"

"Look, she'll just assume I did something wrong and it'll turn into a thing. And she's a single mom, remember? Let's not make her life more difficult."

It was easy to play the single mother card with pretty much anyone. Other kids, their parents, teachers. Anyone I might want to evoke pity from.

It wasn't that I cared my dad was MIA and always had been. I really didn't. Sometimes, I try to imagine a more traditional family for us. And I can't. It seems like if there was another parent in the mix, it would just be messy and complicated.

Ma worked full time. Sometimes during the holidays she picked up seasonal work to get some extra money. I did what I needed to do and got to do what I wanted to do.

If I did the dishes, took out the trash, and folded the laundry, plus homework, don't forget, I pretty much had free rein. Especially since Eric was out of the house now. Total freedom.

Plus, a lot of nights, if my mom was working, Debbie's mom or Mel's mom took pity on me and invited me to dinner. I could eat, hang out, and leave whenever I wanted. Just hightail it away to the silence of my house at will.

I got all the perks of being the kid of a single parent without any of the actual sadness.

"—something bad?"

I realized I'd checked out. I blinked myself back to Mel's worried voice. "Sorry, I dropped the phone. What?"

"I said what if he's up to something? You know, something bad?"

"He wouldn't try that with you two standing there. People like that are usually a little . . . slicker," I said.

"Maybe." She didn't sound convinced.

"Go shower," I said. "I have to do my homework."

It was a lie. My homework was totally done. I just didn't want to talk anymore.

"Over and out," Mel said.

I hung up without reply. That drove her crazy, too.

There was a knock on the door. My mother poked her head in before I could even answer.

"Trash, young lady."

"Shit, I forgot."

"Dorrie!"

"Sorry. *Crap*, I forgot."

She rolled her eyes at me. "As if I'm not aware you cuss like a sailor."

I winked at my mother, in the mood to push some buttons tonight. Maybe it was the rush from my great escape from Mr. Frank. "I learned from the best."

She hmphed. "Trash, now. Then lights out soon. School night."

I saluted my mother. "Aye aye, Linda."

"That's Mom to you."

"If you insist."

I dragged the giant metal can to the curb. I wasn't sure if we'd disposed of a body or what, but it weighed a ton.

I stood at the curb, catching my breath and shoving the lid down to make sure it stayed on.

The hair on the back of my neck tingled. My breath caught.

I looked up quickly. Just in time to catch Mr. Frank stepping back from his bay window.

Blue flickering TV light danced against the windowpanes. He hadn't been fast enough. I'd caught him peeking. Caught him watching me.

Again.

CHAPTER 3

"HE WAS OUT THERE THIS morning." Debbie pushed her front wheel into the bike rack and left it. She never locked it up. One day we were going to come out of school and the fucking bike would be gone.

"So?"

"He was like . . ." She looked up into the bright October sky and sighed. "I don't know. Rummaging?"

I snorted. "Rummaging? For?"

She shrugged. "I have no idea. He was under the fig tree where the ball went yesterday. Like he was going to find something? Like you'd left something behind."

I don't know why but that spooked me a little. My skin bristled.

"And then Dandy went *insane* and I had to drag him back inside. He was barking his ass off. All that drool flying. I swear, I don't know why my parents can't fall in love with a less drooly breed of dog."

"He's majestic," I said.

"And wet."

That made us both crack up. "I have no idea what Mr. Frank was doing. Maybe he thought I messed up his lawn. Maybe he was combing the grass."

This made her laugh harder and then she was off and running about whether or not David Gambino liked her. Did he? No, he couldn't. But she kept catching him staring, so maybe? No. Yes? Maybe!

It was ridiculous, but I just nodded along as if it was the beat to a good song.

"I'm sure he does," I tossed out for good measure.

The words came out of my mouth, but my mind was wandering around Mr. Frank's backyard, pretending to look, wondering what the hell he thought he'd find.

The ball had hopped the fence. I had hopped the fence. I got the ball. I ran out of there when things got weird.

What was he going to find?

I don't know why it bothered me so much knowing there wasn't anything to find anyway. And yet—it rolled through my mind all damn day. The idea of him inspecting the place where I'd been filled me with irrational anger.

I'm not stellar at math as it is, especially if it has the alphabet in it, but my brain was definitely a million miles away now. More so than usual.

"Doris?"

I looked up. "Sorry?"

"I asked if you had solved for X." Ms. Edwards tapped her toe. It was enclosed in a very pointy shoe. I wondered if they pinched her toes. I mean, they had to. Right?

"No. Sorry. I have a—" I put my head down, rubbed my forehead. I was hot again. My skin was too small, my insides too big.

"Doris?"

"Yeah, sorry. I have a headache. I'm just—"

Then the heat was almost unbearable, and my head hit the desk with a *thunk*.

The next thing I knew, Mrs. Nichols, the nurse, was waving a penlight in my face and shoving Gatorade at me the moment my eyes opened.

"Are you okay, Doris?"

"I would be if everyone would call me Dorrie," I snapped. Then I chugged the Gatorade like a pro football player. It was disgusting. The color of pee and not quite sweet but not quite salty.

She frowned.

"A little respect please, young lady."

Respect is earned. I didn't say it, but I wanted to.

My mother burst in then with a wild-eyed look. She looked like our old dog when he thought someone had food.

"Dorrie?"

"I'm fine."

She looked at the nurse, who gave a noncommittal shrug. "She appears fine."

"Should I take her to the—"

"No," I said.

"Probably," Mrs. Nichols said with a small smile. I think she was trying to piss me off.

"I didn't eat breakfast," I said to my mother, cutting off the older woman. "You know what that does to me."

"Yes, and I know I've told you a million times to eat."

It was my turn to shrug. "I wasn't hungry. I'm fine. It was just a moment."

Mrs. Nichols seemed to have lost interest in the whole thing.

She was busy typing a report on her giant dinosaur of a typewriter. It was manual, no less. Every time she struck a key her whole desk went *thud*. It shook me. Filled my bones. Made me want to grab the monster and toss it through the window out into the picturesque fall landscape.

Instead, I put my head down again. "Ma, can we just go home? I'll take something for my head, eat something, lay down. Can we? Please?"

"Let's go."

We had to go collect my stuff from my class and my locker. Everyone stared. Deb gave me a finger wave. Melissa was in Gym. She'd be pissed that she missed all the hoopla.

~

—*feel the devil walking next to me . . .*

My mother turned the radio off and I stopped singing mid-song.

"I have to go back to work. I'll drop you at home. You make sure you eat something, and you *stay there, Doris!*"

"Okay, Jesus, you don't have to yell."

"Language."

"How is Jesus bad language? It's in the Bible about a billion times."

My mother pressed her lips together so tightly they nearly disappeared. I had the wild urge to laugh and had to bite my tongue to stop it.

"Just promise me you're going to behave, Dorrie."

"Of course, I always do."

She eyed me again.

"Why are you suddenly so worried about me not doing what I'm supposed to? I've been a latchkey kid forever."

She shook her head and sighed. "I wish you weren't."

"Well Maw-Maw says shit in one hand and—"

"I know what your grandmother says, and I wish she wouldn't!"

I had to laugh then. My grandmother was one of my favorite people ever.

"I worry without me there or Eric. I just worry. I don't know. I know you do what you're told. I mean, for the most part. You are a teenager after all. After what happened—" She cut herself off.

I didn't say anything.

"Just stay home, don't run over to Debbie's or Mellie's or—"

"She prefers Melissa or Mel," I said.

There went her lips again. Gone. I smiled.

"I'll try to remember that. She's been Mellie since she was little."

I nodded. True. I'd give her that.

"Just be safe. And good. I'm just . . ." My mother exhaled slowly, and I suddenly felt bad for her. "I'm worried. I don't know why. I just worry is all."

"I'm fine. It's fine. I'll make a sandwich and watch MTV," I said.

"Oh boy," my mother said. But she laughed.

CHAPTER 4

I DIDN'T MAKE A SANDWICH and watch MTV. I made a sandwich and watched Mr. Frank's front door. I finally saw him emerge around one o'clock, car keys in hand.

I watched him get in, drive away, and then I waited. I waited about ten minutes to be sure he didn't come back. That he wasn't going to return because he'd forgotten his wallet or something.

Next door was Debbie's house, but her mother's car was gone. I knew her dad was at work, and she, of course, was at school. The only one there would be Dandy. And Dandy the dummy might not even bark because he knew my scent. Debbie told me once that if he knows the person he doesn't bark. He just sits and cries softly because he wants to see the person on the other side of the door.

I put my house key in my pocket and locked the door behind me. Then, spooked, I unlocked it and simply pulled the door shut. Just in case I needed to make a speedy entry.

Worry wormed through me but only for a second. Then a strange warm sense of ease burrowed into my bones and I walked across the street toward his house like I owned it.

I waited at the foot of his first set of steps. Every house had three concrete steps to a landing. Then three more concrete steps to the front walk that led to the front steps of the home itself.

It always seemed like an excess of steps to me. Especially in the winter when they were icy and had to be navigated, but it was what it was.

I stood there to see if anyone would come. When no one did, I went up the three steps, stood on the landing for a moment, then went up the second set of steps. I stood on the front walk regarding the steps to his porch, painted a utilitarian green like the porch itself.

My skin tingled. I followed the walk around to the side gate and lifted the latch. Inside the yard, beneath the trees, it was cooler. Chilly.

It felt nice on my skin.

I inhaled the scent of a crisp fall and listened. Birds. The sound of squirrels or maybe chipmunks in the brush. The sound of chatter from his house.

I walked over and peeked in the window closest to the ground. I had a clear shot through the small, neat kitchen. I could see the TV on in the living room. A fairly large model atop an old floor model. It was running a game show.

Had he left it on to give the appearance that someone was home? To fake out a possible intruder?

Me?

I don't know why I thought that. It was silly. I was a kid. He was a middle-aged man. Why would he want me to think he was home when he wasn't?

I stared for a moment longer and then returned to the scene of the crime. The tree where I'd found the ball. It was a low-hanging tree. Almost forming a canopy over the area where the ball had landed.

I found nothing. A flat shoe print told me it wasn't sneakers. Probably Mr. Frank's dress shoes. What looked like him running his finger through the fine dirt beneath the tree. A pinecone here, a stick there. Nothing nothing *nothing* worth poking around for.

Heat across my face again. A tingling. And then a sudden sense of dread, so hollow and so low, I felt like I'd bottomed out.

I sank to my hands and knees, utterly aware I was once again ruining the knees of my jeans.

"What were you looking for?"

I got myself together and sat back on my haunches.

I heard it before I saw it. The petite, hesitant meows. One of the neighborhood strays must have had a litter.

I pinpointed the sound and found it walking toward me. Slowly. Still wobbly on its tiny little legs. It stumbled and righted itself—determined. The epitome of adorable.

I called it over, beckoning with my hands. When it finally got to me, I scooped it up. So small it would have fit in a teacup.

"What are you doing out here?" I asked. "Where's your mama?"

It meowed again, small blue eyes still cloudy from newness. I stroked the top of its head and thought.

"What is he doing? Why is he focused on me?"

A quick sharp meow and I realized I was petting too hard. I backed off.

"He's always been weird but it's freaking me out," I whispered.

A squeak.

"I don't like it. At all," I hissed, the autumn wind rocking the tree branch above my head.

I heard the snap before I realized what I was doing. Then it was there, slumped in my hand. A line of shit running from its ass. A limp neck where a limber one had just been.

I waited. Waiting for the horror or the sadness or the pity or even the sorrow.

Nothing.

Not one of those emotions showed up.

Just the thought pick-pick-picking in my head.

What did he want? Why was he so nosey? Why me? Why focus on me? What was this all about?

I was surprised at myself in a distant way. Shocked at my lack of reaction or feelings.

I sat in the dirt and waited. The birds stopped singing, the few lone crickets did too. The neighborhood sounded gone—deserted, abandoned.

Then I flung the kitten carcass over the fence into Debbie's yard. If things went my way, they'd blame it on Dandy.

CHAPTER 5

"YOU KNOW THAT NURSE CALLED me at work," my mother said. She'd put a bag of popcorn in the giant humming microwave. That was her dinner.

I was watching some stupid sitcom on TV and she was hovering around me like a deranged hummingbird.

"She did? What did she say?"

"That you were less than respectful." My mother's mouth had narrowed down into a line again.

"So was she."

"Dorrie!"

"What?"

"You should—"

"What? Pretend I'm in kindergarten? Make believe that adults are always right? Or pretend when I'm not up to it?"

My mother opened her mouth, but I rushed on.

"You know I had just been sent to the nurse's office because I fainted, right?"

"I do." She was using that cautious voice she employed when I got worked up.

That pissed me off more.

"So, do you think, Ma, that someone who's just fainted might not be feeling completely great?"

"I do—"

"Good, because that was me. I'd fainted. I was freaked out. I was trying to figure out what was going on and Nurse Ratched was barking orders at me."

My mother shook her head and tsked, but that was the extent of it.

"I will admit, Marcia Nichols can be a bit . . . brisk. I had a few run-ins with her when Eric was in school."

"And?"

"She's annoying." She shoved a handful of popcorn in her mouth and pushed the bowl my way. I begrudgingly took a small handful, shook it, dropped it in my mouth.

"So, there you go," I said, confused by what seemed like a victory.

"I'm bringing it up because I'm wondering if some of your attitude lately is due to what happened."

"Ma!" I barked.

"Sit!" she said.

I hadn't realized I was standing until she said it. I dropped back down to our ugly ass brown and mustard-colored sofa.

"I'm concerned about you. Some of what you're experiencing could be . . . trauma. Do you know what that is?"

"Yes, Ma. I'm not re—"

Her mouth narrowed down.

"Stupid," I amended. She hated that word, and so did I honestly. It was habit.

"Trauma can cause a lot of things and it's entirely reasonable you might be traumatized after what happened."

There was that phrase again.

"I'm fine," I said. My heart pounded. My skin tingled. My face burned.

"You were here alone," she said, looking sad.

"Yes, I know."

"They broke in," she said.

"Yes! I know! I was here!"

"Alone."

"Yes! Alone!" I shouted.

I wanted to run but this was my mother and I knew she'd follow me. Instead, I sat on my hands to keep from clawing at my skin. It itched.

"They broke in and trashed the place and locked you in—"

"A fucking closet!" I yelled at her, suddenly so angry I wanted to smack her.

Eric had moved out, she was at work, and I was here alone.

There were three of them. It was over a year ago and I just wanted to forget it.

"They could have—"

"But they didn't!" I screamed.

Rage seethed through me. Everything I wanted to say danced on the tip of my tongue.

And yet here I am, still alone all the time, Ma . . .

If Eric hadn't deserted us . . .

If my father was even distantly in my life . . .

If, if, if.

I thought they could have killed me, but my mother, she meant they could have raped me. That always baffled me how people said things like, *Well, they killed her but at least she wasn't raped.*

Her vagina was unmarred, but she had ceased to exist? Eradication was better than violation?

I was shaking and I forced myself to still.

"I'm just saying maybe you should talk to someone."

"Maybe. But not tonight. And not you."

She looked hurt and I waited to feel bad. It didn't happen. My body ached, my head too. I wanted to punch my mother square in the face and that scared me. All because of some asshole nurse and her hurt feelings.

"Dorrie—"

"Can we just eat popcorn and watch whatever the hell this show is?"

She studied me for a long moment.

In that moment I recalled that kitten going limp and cold in my hands.

She nodded and sat back, turning her attention to the sitcom and its obvious laugh track.

I went upstairs and closed myself in the bathroom for a moment, my anger boiling so high I wasn't sure what to do. I stared at her candle on the back of the toilet. Some floral stuff. My mother burned it on the rare occasion when she got to soak in the tub.

I THINK I'M ALONE NOW

I picked up the matches. Without thinking, I lit one. I put the match on my tongue and closed my mouth. I heard the sizzle, smelled the sulfur, felt warmth but no pain.

No pain at all.

I left the bathroom and went back to sit dutifully with my mother for a little bit before escaping to my room.

CHAPTER 6

DEBBIE WAS CRYING.

"What's up?" I asked Melissa when I got to the bus stop.

It was raining a little so the bus was the way to go. I found I liked the feel of the rain against my face and in my hair.

I'd slept for shit. My dreams kept waking me and when I sprang to consciousness I could hear (and feel) the snap of the kitten's neck.

Turned out that's why Debbie was crying.

"She asked her mother if she could stay home and her mom said no," Mel whispered to me as we waited.

Debbie was doing that thing she did where she was upset so she sequestered herself from us and wouldn't let us help or empathize. Then in a day or two she'd blame us all for not caring.

I couldn't wait.

"Hmm," was all I managed.

"Her mother said it wasn't like it was their kitten, just a random kitten."

"True," I said.

Melissa flashed me an odd look and then went on. "But her mom doesn't know that she's been slipping it food on the sly."

"Ah," I said. "Working her way up to asking to keep it?"

Melissa nodded. "Probably. You know she's been dying for a cat for a while."

I nodded. "Yep."

"She'd even named it."

"What?"

"Angel," she said.

It was everything in me not to laugh. What a dumb name for a cat.

When I was little, I'd gotten a hamster named Daisy. I remembered thinking an animal had to look like its name for some reason. It bothered me, secretly, that she wasn't yellow, but instead it was white and tan. It bothered me even more when a few weeks later the weather turned warm and Daisy suddenly grew balls. Turned out she was a he and the balls dropped when it got hot.

My mother insisted we take it to the pet store, thinking something was wrong. Neither of us knew what was happening. When the poor clerk said, "Those are ... testicles, ma'am." My mother cackled like a lunatic and I followed suit, not quite getting it.

She explained on the way home and my whole response was: "Eew. Gross."

A few months after he had another growth. This time a tumor. A big one. And Daisy became a bald patch of dirt in the backyard not long after.

I had cried.

Why hadn't I cried for the kitten?

"The bus is coming," Darlene said. She lived two streets over and always—*always*—had on a Care Bears shirt. She also had braces and a lazy eye.

She was okay.

The bus pulled up and, sniffling, Debbie climbed on first. I could tell she was going to milk this for all it was worth.

I glanced back through the rain and saw him. Mr. Frank. Standing on his porch. Watching me.

~

I didn't hear a damn thing in History. I didn't hear anything in Home Ec either. I burned a pan of brownies and my partner was pissed.

"Sorry," I mumbled to Rachel as I scooped up my backpack and purse. "Tell Mrs. H. it was my fault. I'll back you up."

She rolled her eyes and grabbed her own stuff, eager to be free of the scorched smell and of me.

All I could focus on was Mr. Frank and trying to figure out what his deal was with me.

On top of that, why the fuck did I care?

I had a headache very much in the middle of my fucking head. Like a glowing ember buried way down in my brain that was smoldering.

Rummaging, I found the bottle of Tylenol I kept in my purse and swallowed three at the water fountain with a gulp of stale metallic-tasting water.

"You okay?"

I stood up too fast and my head swam. Debbie stood there chewing on the end of her sweatshirt tie. A habit I found annoying and disgusting. It was soggy, so she'd been gnawing on that thing all day.

"Fine. A headache. You okay?"

She nodded but gave a small sniffle. Couldn't pass up that chance for sympathy.

"Yeah. I'm okay."

"Did you even know that cat?"

Her eyes got watery, but I had to give it to her, she didn't cry. "I fed it sometimes. I wanted to take it in and keep it as a house cat. Hadn't found the nerve to ask my mom yet. I knew she'd talk about Dandy and how he'd freak out and . . ." Her words petered out and she shrugged. "I guess it was true."

I shut my eyes and remembered the neck snapping. Remembered the dull thud as it hit the dirt on the other side of Mr. Frank's fence and landed in Debbie's yard.

Frank's face popped up in my mind's eye like a photograph. I focused on his eyes. The eyes were dark and deep and probing. His eyes were intrusive and relentless.

My stomach rolled over with a wave of nausea.

"Let's go. Lunch time," Melissa said, appearing out of nowhere. She grabbed my arm and Debbie's and then hustled us to the cafeteria to tell us about Sharon Glass, who bled through her jeans in Math class.

Ugh. I wanted to go home.

CHAPTER 7

BUT HOME WAS NO BETTER. There was a list on the kitch-en counter of chores I was supposed to do before "plunking down in front of the TV" as the note put it.

"I have homework, too, mother," I said to the note.

I folded the load of clean kitchen towels, put them away, loaded the dishwasher, and put fresh sheets on my bed and hers. By then it was dusk, and I was starving.

The TV had been on the whole time, of course. I played it to keep me company. Not too loud. It had been too loud the night those guys had come. If it was too loud I couldn't hear the noises of the house.

I glanced at the front door because thinking about them con-jured the remembrance of them and that was stressful.

A cold rain had started outside as I'd gotten off the bus and now it was harder. I could hear it pounding our aluminum awnings. Oc-tober rain is always the most chilling for some reason.

Some of the neighbors had their Halloween decorations up al-ready. I was a little jealous. I made myself some tomato soup and a grilled cheese, managing to only scorch one side of it. It was a fine meal along with a sleeve of Ritz crackers and a cold Coke from the fridge.

I watched a rerun of an old black-and-white show and then went in the basement to see if I could find our Halloween decorations.

The popcorn-plastic bat and ghost were front and center in the back room that held the hot water heater and the washer and dryer. The shelves around it held a bunch of our crap. Halloween and Christmas decorations, old tools, some of my mother's discarded arts and crafts projects, and more.

I pulled the two decorations down and then stared at the mess until I saw the cardboard box labeled HALLOWEEN in my mother's neat handwriting.

Top shelf. Of course.

I got on a chair and managed to snag it with my fingertips. I dragged it forward until it was easier to grab. Once I'd gained my prize, I popped the flaps. There was a cloth witch with a broom we hung from a tree, a papier-mâché ghost I'd made in Girl Scouts before I insisted on quitting the troop. Some black, silver, and orange garland my mom had found at a five and dime. Plus, an old scarecrow we made with my little kid clothes a hundred years ago and still put out every year.

I'd decorate. That would prove I wasn't a couch potato.

My homework could wait.

I put the ghost and the bat in the box and made my way up the basement steps, managing not to plummet down them with the oversized box.

Flipping the porch light on, I wondered how wise it was to try this in the rain. I finally decided the rain seemed to be staying off the porch, so I should be okay.

I wired the bat and the ghost decorations on the poles on either side of the front steps. They were instantly wet and so was I, but they were made of plastic so that wasn't a big deal.

Brushing my hair back, I shivered and zipped up my sweatshirt. I put the scarecrow in one of the chairs on the front porch. Once we had pumpkins, one would be nestled between his legs and he'd hold it.

I managed the garland despite the wind and then went to hang the cloth witch from the hook my mother kept windchimes on in the summer.

The witch was instantly ripped from my hand in a gust of wind and flew out into the yard.

"Shit!" I scrambled after her, not wanting to get blamed for losing one of my mother's homemade decorations. She didn't do much crafting now, but she'd had quite a phase a few years back, and the witch, even I had to admit, was pretty cool.

"Oh, come here, witchy poo," I growled as I chased her.

Luck was not on my side because the wind caught part of her billowy cape again and tossed her up in the air. I lunged for her, but missed, managing only to touch the tip of her cloth boot as she drifted toward the road.

"Fuck, fuck, fuck," I said because I could. My mother wasn't there, and I was going to be in deep shit if this thing got lost or worse—if someone ran over it with a car.

As if on cue a car zoomed down our road, its headlights were blind white eyes in the now purpling dark.

The witch hit a bush. I thought I'd gotten lucky. The hag was snagged.

I laughed crazily at the thought and plucked her from the bush just as the wind picked up again and she was ripped from my grip.

"Damn it!" I screamed at the silver rain.

And then there she was in the road and I was bending to snatch her up. The wind had other ideas. It was playing a game with me and I was losing.

Her final destination was against the front tire of a sedan. I bent to get her only to see her leg stretch out.

"No, no," I said. "Not this time you wit—"

"I have her, Doris. You can let go. She won't get away."

Cold water seemed to trickle down my spine and it wasn't rain.

I looked up into Mr. Frank's grim face illuminated only partially by the streetlights.

I let go of the witch as he stood.

CHAPTER 8

I BACKPEDALED A STEP, NOT sure what to do. Anger and fear warred inside me. I'd always kind of rolled my eyes at Mr. Frank. It had been other neighborhood kids that feared him. I'd always recognized him for what he was. A somewhat lonely, very strait-laced man who liked his yard nice. He and his wife hadn't had kids that I knew of, so they didn't want them traipsing through the house.

I remember his wife had always baked cookies at Halloween and tried to give them out. But somehow her husband's urban legend-level reputation squashed her efforts.

Her cookies were usually only accepted by the smallest of children, kids from other neighborhoods, or the parents of kids on this block. Then shoved hastily into their child's trick-or-treat bag.

The anger I felt was no stranger to me. I felt it often. The fear was an unwelcome intruder.

I wiped my wet dirty hands on the seat of my jeans and then mentally kicked myself. My mother was going to have a fit. I should just set these jeans on fire and get it over with.

"I . . ." I half-heartedly reached a hand out and then dropped it.

"You're going to get yourself killed," Mr. Frank said. "Running in the street that way."

"I couldn't let it get away," I said. "It's my mom's. She made it. It—"

He pushed it toward me.

I flinched.

He regarded me stoically and then pushed it toward me again.

I forced myself not to react. When it was close enough to me to grab the end, I did. I was taking this witch from him like I was some feral animal accepting food. Not as if I'd lived across the street from him my whole life.

"Are you okay, Doris?"

The rain was running down the back of my neck, cold and miserable.

"I'm wet. And cold."

He nodded. He too was wet. And maybe cold. It occurred to me this was a completely bizarre scenario and why was it happening?

Why hadn't he just thrust it at me and left? Scolded me for running in the street? Asked after my mom and then disappeared? Why were we out here on the sidewalk in front of his house, me crouched and tense like I was going to bolt out into the street all over again?

I clutched the sopping wet witch.

"Beyond that," Mr. Frank said.

"Beyond what?" I blinked rainwater out of my eyes.

"Beyond wet and cold. Beyond physically. How are you?"

"I'm fine," I said. What else would I say?

"Since the . . ." He hesitated then.

I felt dread pool in my fingertips and toes. My face felt cold. I didn't want to talk about that. Not now. Not ever. It was over, and I wanted it to stay that way.

"I'm fine, thanks."

"Did they hurt you?"

"No," I said hastily.

Hadn't he talked to my mother about this? Why ask me? A kid?

The only thing that night that had hurt was the realization I was completely and utterly on my own. As usual.

It was me and me alone. We didn't even have a fucking dog anymore.

After it was all said and done, I'd asked my mother for a new one. A big one. But she'd said no.

Can you believe that? She said no. To me getting some companionship. Some protection.

I felt my fingers bunch and clench her beloved witch. I felt part of it tear in my hand. It had survived its wind sail across the road and here I was damaging it.

Good.

She deserved it.

"Have you been sad?"

I blinked. Was he nuts?

"Have you been angry?" he pushed.

I stood quickly. I'd been stepping on one of the witch's legs and when I rose, I ripped it from the body.

Good.

That was my first thought. My second was, "Shit," which I said aloud.

"Doris—"

"I have to go!" I blurted. "I left the oven on."

It was a lie, and I was pretty sure we both knew it, but he nodded once.

I grabbed the witch's leg and ran out into the darkness, rain hitting my face, heart pounding.

When I glanced over my shoulder, Mr. Frank was still squatting there, watching me.

Was he some sort of child predator? Like they talked about on *60 Minutes* and *20/20*? Was he crazy? Lonely? Why was he fixated on me? And why did I feel like he could see things inside me even I couldn't?

At home, I put the witch in the kitchen sink. Then I went and took a long hot shower, pulled on some sweatpants and a sweater. I found a pair of Eric's old socks and shoved my feet into them. They were shapeless, wool, and way too big for me, but it comforted me. The sense of my brother there.

Then I went in my mother's room to find her sewing box. Inside, she had a package of safety pins. I grabbed a few of the big ones and went down to reattach the leg.

Witchy Poo had drip dried a bit. Once her leg was back on, I took her out front and hung her in her rightful place.

I was on the sofa eating Doritos and drinking an Orange Crush when my mother came home.

"You decorated!" she said.

I nodded. "Yes, I did. I ripped your witch. I'm sorry."

She ruffled my hair. "It's okay. Hungry?"

I shook the Doritos bag at her.

"For actual food?"

"What did you have in mind?"

"I could order us a pizza," she said.

"Sold."

CHAPTER 9

I WOKE UP. IT WAS still raining. I could hear it. The streetlights threw streaks of cold white light across my bedroom walls.

My mother had bought me a print for the wall of a Pierrot clown sitting on the moon. The thing was spooky as hell, and half illuminated in the darkness of my room it hadn't gotten any less so.

I pictured Mr. Frank over there staring out his window. Staring at my room. Knowing I was in here.

What the hell was wrong with me? Was paranoia part of hormones too?

I glanced at my alarm clock. 3:28 a.m. Hours before I had to get up to go to school. Why was I awake?

I shut my eyes, picturing the rain. Trying to lull myself back to sleep. When the wind would whip I could hear the whiskery sound of the witch blowing on the porch below my room. It was a nylon kind of sound. Like a kite swaying in the wind or a windbreaker.

The sounds were lulling me, and I could feel myself drifting. The heaviness of sleep settling on my limbs like a cat.

Something slid along my shoulder. Gripped it. Squeezed.

A hand stroking me. My mother used to do that. She would put her hand on me and pet me like the dog. It always made me sleepy.

31

Another stroke. The rasp of nails on my t-shirt. I jolted, reaching up. A hand. My fingers touched fingers. Fingernails. Knuckles.

I wasn't dreaming.

Crying out, I pushed up, flailing, the bedcovers catching and binding me.

I felt those fingers brush my face, slip through my hair, and scrabble at my lips.

A scream broke out of me and I started to kick and punch. Something was in bed with me. Someone.

I kicked my feet out, inching back on the mattress, and then I was falling. My ass hit the floor. The fall knocked the wind out of me so hard my lungs burned.

The lights came on, brilliant and blinding.

"Dorrie! Dorrie!"

I lashed out and heard my mother grunt.

My mother.

It was my mother.

She managed to get my face uncovered, my hair streaked across my vision and she brushed it away.

"It's a dream. You're having a dream. It's okay. Dorrie— Dorrie!" She shook me so hard my teeth clacked together and then I froze.

I looked up at my bed. It was a double bed on an antique frame. Most of the bedding was on the floor with me where I lay currently tangled. The pillows were askew. One side of the bed butted up to the wall.

The bed was empty.

I leaned forward and sobbed like I was dying. I saw beneath my bed. Some shoes, some dust bunnies, a few books, my flute case.

No person. Nothing with fingers or nails or hands to reach out and molest me in the dark.

"Dorrie?"

"Ma?"

She pushed the hair out of my face. "Dream," she said.

"No," I said. I shook my head.

She pulled me in and hugged me despite the fact I'd basically punched her in the face.

"Yes, honey. It's happened a few times since—"

Night terrors. Once even sleep paralysis. At least that's what the doctor called it.

But that was so long ago, and I was over it. Done with it. It was almost a year ago.

"Memories can cause issues," my mother was starting in her sing-song understanding voice.

I couldn't. It nauseated me to think of hearing her out.

"I'm going down to the sofa. I want to let the TV run. I want—"

"But it's a school night."

"Ma, I can lay here and not sleep at all, or I can listen to a crappy cable channel until it's time to get up for school."

She sighed. "There is literally nothing on TV right now."

"It's light and noise."

"You want to sleep with me?"

"Ma," I said, snorting.

She laughed. "Too grown up for that, I see. Fine. Go down, but just for tonight."

"Just for tonight."

The sofa was tucked in against the back wall. It was too narrow for anyone but me to be on it. I wanted that comfort. A high back, end tables crowding me in, the light of a TV keeping anything that might want to touch me at bay.

CHAPTER 10

MY EAR ITCHED. WAY DOWN deep. And I was prone to wax. My mother once had me at the pediatrician thinking I was going deaf. She was borderline hysterical when Dr. Jack looked in my ear, inserted something long that looked like a very thin silver spoon, and scooped out a huge wad of wax.

"Doris, can you hear me now?"

I jumped, he seemed so loud after weeks and weeks of muffled hearing.

"This might be the problem," he said good naturedly, holding the small instrument out to my mother.

"My god, Dorrie! Do you ever clean your ears?"

He'd laughed then, and I'd liked him even more for it.

"That has nothing to do with it. Some people are prone to a waxy build-up. Doris seems to be. If it happens again, bring her in, we'll Roto Rooter those ears and she'll be good as new."

With that, he'd handed me a lollipop, dropped me a wink, and left.

My ear felt clogged again. Muffled like that long-ago time. I stuck my pinky finger in there and wiggled it. Often, this could dislodge a clump of wax and then I could scrape it out with my pinky nail.

It didn't work. A rustling sounded in my ear. It made me feel claustrophobic and helpless.

I did it again, digging my finger in there, trying to work the blockage free. I used my nails next, desperate.

The whispering sound grew louder. A dead leaf rustling deep in my ear canal. I grunted, digging, pushing, trying to yank my finger out quickly to work up some suction.

The sound filled my head.

I cried out, pulled again, and a wad of reddish wax burst free.

I laughed. Relief flooded my body, making me feel weak. I felt another release of pressure and touched the side of my head. It was wet. I looked at my hand. A stain of reddish-brown ooze.

Another pop in my ear. Another fresh rush of wetness.

Now it wouldn't stop. It didn't stop.

A river of gunk spilled out of my ear and I rushed to the hallway where a mirror hung on the wall.

My face was coated and dripping on the left side. It was thick and it stank. I wiped it away fruitlessly with my hand. Then I used my sleep shirt. I wiped and wiped and every time I did my ear vomited out a fresh gush of fluid.

Somehow, I'd broken the seal and now it was flowing out of me. Rust-red and putrid smelling. I covered my ear with the palm of my hand and then felt a new surge of pressure and then the release. I knew it was coming but tried so hard to hold it in.

This time, what flowed between my tightly clenched fingers was black. Black as night. Black as tar.

It oozed between the seams of my fingers and down the back of my hand.

Frantically, I pressed the plug of wax back in my ear. Trying to work it in. Trying to stop the flow.

It failed, wetness rushing up and around it.

I stuck my finger in and that failed.

I found a pen and tried the non-writing end. It failed.

Finally, I shoved the pointed end in, trying to wedge it deep, fill in that space and stop it.

A roaring filled my head and I sobbed and sobbed.

The flow wouldn't cease. There was no end to it.

The blackness in me kept oozing and the roar in my head grew so loud I screamed.

I THINK I'M ALONE NOW

Then the world was tilting, and I was colliding with rocks and my eyes flew open and my mother looked down at me on the living room floor as I clutched my perfectly fine head in my hands.

"I see the TV helped," she said.

CHAPTER 11

"DO YOU THINK IT'S BECAUSE they're out?"

I stabbed a sausage link with my fork. I kept rubbing my ear. The one that had let loose like a fire hose in my dream. I kept plucking at it and poking at it because I was convinced it was suddenly going to rupture and fill my world with goo. Or blood.

"Dorrie!"

"What?" I barked.

My mother looked at me. Her cool hand slid over mine to cover it. "Do you think it's because they're out?"

She enunciated each word as if I were hard of hearing.

Which reminded me of my dream and made me rub my ear harder.

"Do I think what is because who is out?" I asked, to placate her.

My mother exhaled mightily and sat back in her chair. She seemed more than a little frustrated with me.

Get in line.

"The men who broke in. They were released. Did you know?"

I shook my head. "No."

I didn't know why everyone was so upset about these guys. They couldn't hurt me anymore. I wasn't afraid of them. I was once. But not now.

I pushed my fingertip in my ear.

"Are you okay? Do you have an ear infection?"

I hurriedly shook my head. "No. Nope. I'm fine. Just tired."

My mother got up to pour more coffee. I stared at my fingertip, the skin stained amber from my incessant digging.

My head felt heavy and full. Maybe I was getting sick.

I stood up and put my plate on the counter. "I have to get ready."

My mother stared at the plate. "You barely ate anyth—"

"Not hungry," I said, hurrying away.

In the bathroom, I stood, back against the wall, catching my breath. My heart didn't want to calm down. I tried to push on and brush my teeth. Head down, scrub, scrub, scrub.

When I looked up there was a hint of amber at the bottom of my right nostril.

I touched it.

It twitched once and scurried.

I felt it. Riding high and moving swiftly into my sinuses.

"No!"

I exhaled hard through my nose and it reappeared, that amber bit, with little bisected legs and the very end of a carapace.

"Oh fuck, no!" I said.

My voice was low because my anxiety was high.

I grabbed the wiggling end and pulled it out. A roach. A cockroach.

My whole body recoiled at the sight. I sneezed and then I gagged. I dropped it in the sink and it quickly scurried down the drain.

I felt them then. Up there in my nose. I gagged again, felt the tickle and drag way back in my sinuses.

I sneezed over and over again. Roaches flew from my nostril, quickly going down the drain. I turned my head, threw up on the floor, and then sneezed again.

A lone cockroach spun on its back in my puke. It made me puke again.

I was sobbing. My anguish was absolutely overwhelming, and I dropped to the rug.

I sneezed and sobbed and gagged and then my mother was banging on the door and I was screaming and when she came in she dropped to the ground and shook me hard.

Then harder still.

And when I opened my eyes, none of it was there. Just the puke. But no visitor doing the backstroke in it.

No hint of a roach in sight.

Nothing.

Just me and my hysteria and my ever-pounding heart.

"I think we should get you to the doctor. I can call out today. They won't like it but too bad. They'll have to make do without m—"

I forced myself to my feet. My head swam and then it roared all over again, filling with the sound of white noise, the ocean, the void.

"I'm fine, Ma. Go to work. I choked. That's all."

"On what?" she sighed.

I glanced around for an answer.

"Toothpaste," I said. "Went down the wrong pipe."

CHAPTER 12

"WE SHOULD GO TO THE mall after school," Melissa said. "The Limited is having a sale on sweaters. You know, the V-neck ones I like?"

She was the only one of us who had money for Forenza and she loved to subtly rub it in.

"Maybe," I said.

My fingers skated along the tip of my nose, brushed my ear, rubbed at the center of my forehead.

I swore I could still feel them crawling. But it seems they never existed at all.

They were all in my head. While not being literally in my head.

"You okay?" Debbie had finally stopped pouting about the dead kitten.

"Fine."

"You don't look so hot," she poked.

"Headache," I said. "I'll be fine."

"So, do you want to?" Melissa asked. "My mom said if we took the bus out, she'd come pick us up after. We could get pizza at Sbarro."

I shrugged, not really listening. "Maybe."

CHAPTER 13

I USUALLY LIKED THE MALL. The hustle, the bustle. A lot of the stores had Halloween decorations up. It was warm in contrast to the chilly October evening.

Instead of feeling happy, I felt overwhelmed. Everything was too loud. Too bright. Too many people jostling against one another.

Melissa was going on and on about a yellow sweater versus a black sweater and Debbie was giving this dilemma serious consideration.

I was leaning against the wall near a display of acid-wash jeans and denim dresses.

"Dorrie?"

"Hmm?" I had zoned out again.

"What do you think?"

"I think you can afford both of them so why don't you get both of them?"

She looked at me, crestfallen. For just a second, her blue eyes narrowed, and I wanted to scream at her: *Yes! Yell at me! Scream! Pull my hair! Do something other than go on and on and on about which sweater to buy. No one fucking cares!*

Instead of saying any of that I sighed.

Instead of doing any of that, she turned back to Debbie.

It was finally decided that she would indeed get both.

I think she was angry because I had stolen that moment from her. The oh-well-I-guess-I-can't-decide-I'll-just-take-it-all-Melissa special.

I didn't care. I just wanted to go.

But we still had to eat.

Sbarro was packed. The blood red wallpaper with black flocking made it feel like I'd crawled inside my own head.

We all ordered slices—cheese for me, pepperoni for them—and Cokes. We got a corner booth and I slid in last.

It was dark. Like on a first date kind of dark and when I stared out at the mall it looked like I was looking down a long narrow tunnel into light. Like a fish at the bottom of the ocean looking up into the world.

Then he walked by.

Long greasy brown hair pulled back into a scraggly ponytail. Chin whiskers. Lynyrd Skynyrd raglan with faded baggy jeans and Vans. I recognized the walk and the way he rubbed his chin like it constantly itched.

The third guy. The one who had ripped open the closet door. The one who had yanked me out. The one who had been considering something much worse until his buddies convinced him they had to go.

Melissa and Debbie were yammering, picking at their pizza, sipping at their sodas. They'd stopped trying to engage me, and I didn't blame them.

I stood. "Gotta pee," I blurted.

"Eew," Debbie said, snorting.

Melissa shook her head. "Just say you have to go to the ladies' room."

"I'm not a princess, Mel," I said.

I didn't have time to argue. I threw down my paper napkin and headed back toward the restrooms where he was headed.

I saw him push into the men's room and as I passed the trash can with the bussing bins on top, I scooped a serrated knife out of the tumble of dishes.

Somehow, I was on autopilot. Somehow, I was cool as the proverbial cucumber. Somehow, my heart was barely even beating, let alone beating fast.

I pushed into the restroom and saw him there at the urinal, his back to me. Paying no mind because it was just another guy coming in the restroom. I bent low and looked under the stalls. No feet. It was just us.

I flipped the bolt lock, grateful I didn't need a key.

That noise made him look. When he saw me, he laughed.

"Wrong room," he said. "Chicks are next door."

I kept advancing. My hand curled tight around the handle of the knife.

Feeling better than I had in ages, I came up close behind him and jammed the knife into the back of his neck.

I don't know what I hit. I wasn't aiming for anything in particular. I simply buried it to the hilt in the back of him.

His legs buckled, and he went down. He slid to his side then flipped to his back. His dick still hanging out of his fly. Convenient.

Bending, I made quick work of it. The knife was thick and sharp, and it went through his member like butter. There was more blood than I anticipated. He'd fainted long ago, was possibly bleeding out, and I had no time to consider it. I shoved a wad of wet paper towels in his mouth, hoping he'd choke to death on them if he hadn't already died.

His dick lay on the floor like a flesh-colored slug. I stared at it, wondering what would have happened if those boys hadn't talked him out of it. If they hadn't been skittish and worried about someone showing up. I pressed the toe of my sneaker on the tip, leaving a ring of dirty tread mark on it. Then I kicked it across the floor. It didn't go far, too sticky. It rolled to a stop and I turned my back on it coolly. On him, too.

I rinsed my hands in the sink and scrubbed the knife handle with hot water. I had no idea if that would work so I went a step further and dropped it into a big bucket of dirty mop water under the sink.

The water was so murky the knife literally disappeared as if I'd tossed it into a swamp.

I unlocked the door, peeked out, and seeing the coast was clear, I hustled back to the table.

"There you are! We have to meet my mom out by the Farrell's. We're late!"

I grabbed my purse and followed them out. "Sorr-eeee," I said. "I had to poop."

I only said it because it would get a rise out of them.

I THINK I'M ALONE NOW

I smiled when they both shrieked "Gross!" simultaneously.

Inhaling the night air deeply, I realized how fucking good I felt.

In my head I heard "Good girl."

I stopped, cocked my head, listening.

Nothing else. Just the rush of my thoughts and the sounds of a mall parking lot at night.

Loud cars, loud kids, loud horns, and the hiss of rain.

CHAPTER 14

I WAITED FOR THE FULL effect of what I'd done to sink in or bother me. I waited and waited. Then I waited some more.

Nothing.

I sat in the backseat with Debbie, rattling off her Christmas wish list for Melissa's mom. Melissa's wish list was always about four times the length of ours and she usually got all of it and then some.

It had never bothered me before, but somehow, it itched under my skin this year.

I smelled my fingertips. They smelled like cheap bathroom pink soap but under it the smell of pennies. Wet metal. Blood.

I sniffed harder.

"What about you, Dorrie?" Mrs. Reed asked. "Do you know some of what you want already like these two greedy girls?"

I shrugged. "I'd like a new boombox for my room. Mine is held together with tape and prayers."

She laughed at that.

"But that's all I can think of right now."

She made a point to stare at her daughter. "See. That's how it should be. Look, Dorrie has to think about it. Isn't that nice?"

"Dorrie also announced when she came out of the bathroom

that she took so long because she had to poop," Melissa said.

Mrs. Reed wrinkled her nose and I had to stifle a laugh. A mean laugh, at that.

"Well, that isn't as charming, is it?"

I snorted, and she smiled and then the other two went back to all the things they wanted.

I smelled my fingertips and examined my hands every time we stopped at a light to see if I could see any blood. All I saw were red or green or amber streaks across my skin, depending on what color the light was.

Rain dotted the windows and I wondered if anyone was home at my house.

~

No one was home. I opened the door and went right to the fridge. I was suddenly starving, and I hadn't eaten but one bite of my pizza before taking care of the guy in the bathroom.

I found a block of cheese, a sleeve of saltines and sat and ate almost all of them. I washed it down with a cold Coke and then found a bag of M&Ms in the cabinet. I ate two big handfuls and then went up to take a shower.

I let the hot spray rain down on me as I replayed the death scene in my head over and over and over.

I realized that's what it felt like. A movie. Like I had watched it happen. The moment had been no more real than the memory was. A movie on a loop.

The phone was on its final ring when I got out of the shower. I heard the machine cut on and then my mother's voice. And then more of my mother's voice as she left me a message.

"Dorrie, it's Mom."

I rolled my eyes. "Duh. I can hear you."

"I forgot to leave you a note to take the trash to the curb please. And there's not much to eat. Sorry about that. I'll get some groceries soon. I think there's a frozen dinner in there if you want—" A long sigh. "Anyway, I shouldn't be much later. Love you."

I put on my jeans and a sweatshirt and shoved my feet into sneakers. I went out and dragged the trash can to the curb. The rain was light but persistent.

"What did you do?"

I looked up. It took my eyes a moment to adjust. But then I saw him. Standing there on his side of the street. Yelling across to me.

"You've done something. What did you do?"

"Why are you so obsessed with me, Mr. Frank? Why are you watching me? Do I need to tell someone about you? Are you a danger to children?"

The words rolled off my tongue easily. Glib, nasty, tinged with bitterness.

He didn't react the way I thought he would. But I didn't know what the hell was happening.

What was happening to me?

"I'm only a danger to a certain kind of child. And sadly, I'm starting to think that may be you."

I stared at him. Waiting to flee. Waiting to get upset. Instead, I stood there coolly regarding him like he was something foreign stuck to the sole of my shoe.

"What kind of kid is that?" I asked softly. Challenging him.

"A dangerous one."

"Me? Dangerous?" I smiled at him and to my own surprise, took a step toward him.

He took a step back, caught himself, and forced himself to stand still.

We locked eyes under the streetlights. Instead of wanting to flee, my urge was to go at him. And he could tell. His very stance said he knew I was on the verge of charging him like some kind of rabid animal.

The flashes in my head. Knife, blood, skin, mangled flesh, hot water, and cheap pink soap.

The car ride home streaked with red and green and gold in the October darkness. Streaked with lights like some kind of Christmas parade.

He held up his hands like I was a rabid animal.

"You're very sick. And I don't think you realize it. I'd very much like to help you. I've been watching you and—"

"So, you are a pervert?" I laughed.

Somewhere in the night a siren sounded.

"And I think I can possibly help you before it's too late."

"Too late? Like when you get caught molesting a young girl it will be too late."

"I've never molested anyone," he said. He sighed mightily and then put his hand in his pocket. A scattering of silver flew at me. I instinctively reached out and plucked one from the air. I instantly dropped it, my fingers aching, my stomach revolted. I leaned over and vomited all over the curb at my feet.

I stared down until the array of debris came into focus. Religious medals. Saints, the Holy Mother, and the one I'd grabbed—a crucifix.

I started to laugh.

For the first time, a stab of fear sounded deep inside me but didn't seem to touch my exterior.

I saluted him with two fingers. "Later, Mr. Frank. We have to stop meeting this way."

"I'll be seeing you, Doris," he said. There was steel in his voice and a certainty that rattled me.

"It's Dorrie now," I snarled and walked away.

Inside, I locked the door and went to the fridge. I found a pack of sausage at the back of the fridge. I unwrapped the butcher paper and pulled a link out and stood there eating it.

It was only when I was done eating it that I realized it was raw.

I shoved what was left back in the fridge and went to bed.

I heard my mother come in and softly call my name very late, but I pretended to be asleep.

She let me be.

Finally, I did fall asleep. And I dreamed of bloody skin, cutting, streaky streetlights, and a silver rain of religious medals on a black wet street.

CHAPTER 15

I CREPT PAST MY MOTHER'S room carefully since her shift had run late last night. She worked in the filing room at the hospital on the night shift. She got to run files to doctors and nurses in the dead of night.

She also worked at the small corner store part-time when she could fit it in.

Which meant, since she was off today, I'd try to let her sleep. I also didn't feel like answering a million questions.

My sleep had been a big black hole of lost time. Just what I wanted after the night before and the hallucinations that had started my day. That was the only way I could explain the roaches and the ear thing.

Hallucinations.

Maybe it was hormone related.

Wasn't everything?

Out at the curb, I squatted by the now empty trash can with a dustpan. I searched for the medals but found nothing. Either Mr. Frank had retrieved them after I went back in the house or someone had picked them up. Maybe a particularly religious trash man had found himself an early morning surprise.

I put the can back where it went and then went in the kitchen to make myself a piece of toast. I ate it while staring out the front window at Mr. Frank's house.

"Oh, Frank. Are you so very bored that you have to stalk a little girl?"

His wife had been an odd duck. Small, quiet, a little jumpy. She'd always worn a silver cross at her throat and was constantly toying with it.

My mother insisted on dragging me and Eric to church on the holidays. Easter, Christmas, sometimes Thanksgiving. Just a chance to make an appearance.

A part-time Christian as one of the teachers at school so bluntly put it.

They went to the same church, Mr. and Mrs. Frank. And she was always close by him. Her little dark eyes darting this way and that as if she expected someone to jump out at her.

She had died a few years back. Of what, I didn't know for sure. Cancer, I think. Once, Debbie said she thought it was "just of old age" but fifties weren't exactly ancient, so I had to think it was some sort of illness.

I put my plate in the dishwasher and found a Coke. My mom would die if she saw me drinking Coke at breakfast, but what she didn't know wouldn't hurt her.

I managed to grab the phone halfway through its first ring so as not to wake my mother.

"Hey, loser," Melissa said. "Sleepover tonight. Be there or be a bigger loser." Then she guffawed herself into a laughing attack.

I waited. "What time?"

"Six?" It was like I could hear her shrug. "Whenever. Just get here before eight or my mom will spaz out."

"Got it," I said.

A sleepover. Not sure if I was in the mood for one, but it would certainly take my mind off things.

~

Eric turned into Melissa's cul-de-sac. "Got all your shit, kid?"

"I'm hardly a kid," I said. "I turn fifteen in December."

"Whatever, kid. Baby . . . fetus."

I smacked his leg. "Thanks for driving me."

"It's all good. Let Mom sleep."

"All day?"

"I've seen it happen," he said.

I grabbed my bag and my purse.

Eric stopped me. "How are you doing, really?"

I shrugged "Fine. I miss you being there."

"I know. Sorry."

"Don't be."

He didn't let go of me. "But I am."

Melissa's dad walked toward the house, a six-pack in hand. He spotted me and waved.

"Her dad?" Eric asked as I waved back.

"Yup, lucky bitch. She's got one."

I hadn't meant to say it but there it was. A truth rolling off my tongue and landing in the silence of the car with a nearly audible plop.

"Hey, it's . . . complicated."

"Uh-huh. I notice you have a dad. You know who he is and everything."

"Mom didn't stay with your dad because she was raised a certain way and he was into some . . ." Eric petered off.

I nudged him with my elbow. Hard. "Into? Hookers? Drugs? The circus?"

"Some odd stuff."

"Drugs?" I repeated.

"I don't think so, but I don't know. Just odd stuff. She felt like raising you alone was best."

"And how do you know all this? She's always a completely closed book about it."

"I accidentally found her diary and also accidentally read part of it."

I was horrified.

I was intrigued.

Note to self: One day, try to find Mom's diary.

Then Melissa was at her front door waving crazily with her arms like she was trying to guide a 747 in for a landing.

"Gotta go," I said. "Thanks for the ride."

"Call me if you need me," he said, looking way too grown up for my taste. "You know that one guy who was part of the break in? They found him the other day in the bathroom at the—"

"I'll call," I said, and left quickly.

I already knew what he was going to say. I'd been there.

CHAPTER 16

WE'D FINISHED *THE CORSICAN BROTHERS* and an enormous bowl of air-popped popcorn drowned in butter. Melissa's mom had brought us a bunch of two-liter bottles of soda and then had disappeared into her bedroom with a book and a drink.

"I love Cheech and Chong," Debbie said.

"We should get high one day," Melissa said.

I rolled my eyes though neither of them could see me. Coming from a girl who worried about her caffeine intake, getting high seemed over the top.

"That would be fun," Debbie said.

"I can get some," I said barely loud enough to be heard.

There was dead silence from both of them as the VCR clicked to the end of the tape and the unit began to rewind automatically.

"You can? Really?" Debbie rolled to face me. Her long dark hair shielded part of her pale face. She was getting chubby, I noticed. But my mom said that could be puberty. A lot of kids got a bit chunky and then had a growth spurt.

First you go out, then you go up! was one of her favorite reminders after she watched an after-school special with me about anorexia.

I knew that Debbie worried, though.

"Yeah. But we might want to take it easy," I said. "If we try it."

"Because it might be strong?" she asked, wide eyed.

"Because it can make you eat. A lot. And . . ." I tried to act sincere. "You'll want to watch that."

The look of hurt that flashed over her face was so very intense, I felt a shiver run through me. Like pleasure. Like joy. Then a sudden but small stab of guilt. Way down deep.

"From who?" Melissa demanded, arms crossed.

"Eric. Who else? He's old enough to know some people. I know he smokes from time to time. And he lives alone. Plus, he feels guilty for moving out, so I bet I could convince him."

I was full of shit. I had no intention of getting us pot. I was just amusing myself.

Not to be outdone at her own sleepover, Melissa got up and flounced out of the room. She returned with a jug of rum and shook it at us.

"Well, until Dorrie's great drug heist, we can do this."

Debbie sat up and her hand fluttered to her throat. Scandalized!

I did laugh then. I couldn't help myself.

"Pour it up, bartender," I said, sitting up.

Finally, I wasn't so bored. Finally, I didn't want to chew my wrists open to escape them.

When had my friendships soured? When had I?

We had rum and Cokes and started the tape over again. I watched them, my two best friends.

Deliberately trying to get drunk. Why? I had no idea. How does this prove I can't get pot, Mel? How did this solve anything?

But I let them go and I sipped my drink. It was way too strong, the color of iced tea instead of soda.

It didn't take long. We didn't really drink. Once, we had stolen a wine cooler at a cookout and drank it, splitting it three ways.

It hadn't done much but make us burp.

When they were drunk, and I had nursed a third of a drink, I got them to watch another movie. Melissa's mother rented movies for us like it was nothing. My mother rented me one a month. Too expensive.

It wasn't long before they were snoring, and I went to Mrs. Reed's desk and started looking. I found what I wanted and went upstairs to Melissa's room. She had her own bathroom and everything.

I THINK I'M ALONE NOW

I shut the door softly and kept the bathroom light on. Her mother assumed we were downstairs. If I was quiet, I'd be fine.

I opened her closet and got to work.

CHAPTER 17

SCREAMING. SCREAMING, SCREAMING, SCREAMING.
And then more screaming.

I opened my eyes and barely managed to keep myself from screaming too from the shock. They were in Mel's room and I was asleep on a pile of sweatshirts in her bathroom.

The light came on and then Melissa was staring down at me. Her eyes wide, her mouth working but no sound coming out.

Debbie was right behind her. But she looked at me and said, "Dorrie? You okay?"

I rubbed my head and then rubbed it again. It ached, and I felt like I was underwater.

Random flashes came back to me. The movie, the rum, silently moving through the house, digging in the desk and then . . .

Nothing.

Until Melissa held up a handful of colorful ribbons, shook them at me, and growled, "Why?"

"Why what?" I asked, even though staring at those strips of cotton candy colors I knew what she was asking.

"Why did you ruin my fucking clothes!" Melissa shrieked.

Then her mother was there. "Girls, girls! What is all the yelling abou—"

She stopped mid-sentence, looking around, taking in the wreckage and ruin. "Oh, my God. What—"

"Dorrie! Dorrie is what happened!" Melissa shouted, shaking her fist, making the bits of fabric dance and sway.

Mrs. Reed squatted and scooped up scraps of denim, bits of lace, and then finally her wickedly big, ridiculously sharp sewing scissors.

"Dorrie?" she asked.

"I—"

"Dorrie, are you okay?" Debbie repeated.

I shook my head. It ached. Hurt like it was going to split right down the middle and spill my brains out all over the piles of shredded fabric. A wave of nausea swept through me.

"You look green," Debbie said.

I was hot. So fucking hot. My face burned, my hands too, and I expected to see fire shoot from my fingertips they were so hot.

But when I pressed my palms to my face they were freezing cold.

"Dor—" Mrs. Reed stared.

But I was clambering up and onto my knees, gripping the edges of the toilet, hurling my guts up. Heave after heave, emptying what felt like my entire body into the churning water.

The scent of my own vomit made me vomit more. And with every exquisite contraction of my guts to clear themselves, I saw it all. Me lovingly opening her drawers, taking things out, cutting pretty strips from each and every one. Humming while I did it. Letting the soft and delicate bits of debris sift through my fingertips.

Then lying down somehow exhausted and a little ill on the bathroom floor.

While I puked, and Debbie tried to rub my back and hold my unruly hair, Melissa kept on caterwauling.

As if she didn't have the money to replace all this shit.

As if she wasn't the luckiest of us all.

As if anyone cared about her insignificant trauma when she had the world on a platter.

I had a break in the puking and raised my head. I suppressed a smile and made sure to look as miserable as possible.

"I'm sorry, Mel. I'm so sorry. I don't know what came over me."

I made sure to retch here.

"It might . . . I mean it could only have been . . ."

She suddenly looked panicked with her mother standing there watching it all go down.

"It must have been all that rum you gave me," I managed on a spectacular gag.

Then I shoved my head back in the toilet and threw up another rousing batch of bile. I was smiling as I did it.

CHAPTER 18

A FEW DAYS LATER, I was standing by the edge of the front
lawn at school when Karen showed up.

"You okay? I noticed you're not with your normal gang."

I studied her. She sat with us occasionally at lunch, had invited
me to different things. She seemed to want to be friends but me and
Deb and Mel were pretty tight, and we didn't really need a fourth.

But I was bored.

We'd all three been grounded. Melissa most of all. Debbie was
just bummed and not allowed to hang out with either of us for a
week. Mel was furious. I had gotten off the easiest. My mother had
made me fork over my two hundred dollars in savings to help pay
for Mel's clothes. I was supposed to come right home from school.
And that was that.

She was worried the news about one of my attackers coupled
with an unusual incident like drinking had pushed me over the edge.

She knew no one could police me coming home right away and I
knew it too.

"We're all grounded."

"From?"

"Each other," I said, laughing.

She looked very interested.

"Want to come home with me? Have a Coke? See my house?"

I cocked my head. "What's so special about your house?"

She smiled. "I'm down in the city. A rowhome. It's the house where *The Exorcist* was shot."

No, it wasn't. I was a huge fan of that movie and I knew damn well it had been shot in Georgetown in D.C. Not in Baltimore City.

"Really?"

"Yeah. It's really cool and creepy. Three stories. You should come."

I shrugged. What else did I have to do?

"Sure. How are we getting there?"

"My mom works late," she said.

Ditto, Karen. Ditto.

"I take the bus. You okay with that?"

I nodded and shouldered my book bag. "Sure. Let's go."

And off we went. Me and my new buddy Karen.

The bus wasn't crowded, and it didn't take long to get to her stop. We got off and she led me up the brick steps of a rowhome.

The paint around the windows was peeling. Same went for the paint on the transom. She pulled a key from her pocket and unlocked the door.

"Home sweet home."

It was pretty cool. I'd give her that. The front room was a living room. One of the chairs looked like a wicker throne with a huge flared back and arms that were super wide. I ran my fingers over a wall tapestry depicting a moonlit ocean.

I followed her through the dining room and then into a large kitchen with tall ceilings and whitewashed cabinets. The room was painted a cool turquoise and had Batik curtains.

It was all very hippy dippy and colorful.

She opened the fridge and pulled out two frosty cans of Coke. Thank God, I was fearing RC or something equally bad.

Then she surprised me by popping the butter door open and extracting a pack of Kools.

"My mom's. She only smokes a few a day. Says keeping them in the fridge keeps them fresh."

Fair enough.

"It makes it easy for me to help myself," she said, grinning.

Now the question was, was she trying to impress me, or did Karen really smoke?

"Want one?" she asked, offering me the pack.

"Sure," I said.

I mean, when in Rome.

I'd never smoked in my life but found the prospect of doing something that would give my mother a fit quite exciting. I was bored. This would make life less boring.

"Come on."

She led me back to the living room and up the wide staircase.

The second floor had a bedroom dead ahead, one to the left, and a room outfitted as an office that faced the street. A spacious bathroom with a claw foot tub crouched between the two bedrooms.

As I passed the doorway, I saw my own exhausted reflection in the mirror. Pale skin, shadows under my eyes, crazy hair. I looked like hell.

We trudged up yet another staircase to the third floor. A large open area outfitted with an exercise bike, a lot of storage stuff and a section that faced the street that had a huge window and was lush with ferns and other plants.

"My mother." She rolled her eyes. "Ever since my folks got divorced, she has this thing about growing shit. I wish she'd grow some pot. At least that would be productive."

I smiled to let her know I got the joke.

"One more," she said.

"One more what?"

"Staircase."

She led me to a small set of iron steps that led to a trap door. She flipped it up with some effort and daylight wandered in. It was already waning. Purpling at the edges. It would be getting dark soon.

We went up and then we were on the roof. Tarpaper under our feet. I could feel the rolling terrain of the roof as we walked toward the edge.

Speaking of the edge . . .

"Woah!" I said, laughing. "Not very tall is it?"

She grinned again, obviously pleased.

I leaned onto the ledge, my belly flush to the stone it was so low. I looked over and down down down. Vertigo hit me, and I surrendered to it.

She lit her cigarette and handed me the lighter. I lit mine. Menthol. Gross. It tasted like a stick of gum on fire.

I took a shallow puff and then another.

"You come up here all the time?"

Karen nodded. "To smoke. I'm always afraid she'll notice it's smoky when she comes home from work. I don't need the lecture."

I nodded knowingly.

"Your mom work late, too?"

"Often."

"Your dad?"

I shrugged. She went to school with me. Surely, she knew. Everyone did. Once upon a time, when I was younger, people used to make fun of me about my dad. Until they realized I didn't care. It's no fun to taunt people when it doesn't upset them.

"Never knew him."

"Oh man. I'm sorry."

Another shrug from me. "Don't be. It's fine. My mom and I get along fine. My brother and me were tight, but he moved out. His dad would take me with them to fun stuff when I was little. Which was nice."

She nodded along as I talked, smoking her cigarette like a pro.

"Your dad?"

"Moved back to Michigan where he came from once they got divorced. I'm used to it. I go down for most of the summer and for a week of winter break. I miss him, though."

I watched her. Wondering what that felt like. Missing your dad.

We both leaned over and looked to the city street below. The buses belched gray smoke as they traveled. The sky was only a shade lighter than the smoke. The coming darkness crept closer.

Karen wore white on white Tretorns, jeans, and a red sweater. She reminded me of an American flag.

Did she have the Tretorns and the Jordache and the other stuff because of her dad's checks? Because her mom made great money? Because she was spoiled?

I dropped my cigarette. "Shit."

I bent to retrieve it and while down there, grabbed her ankles, hoisted her up and over the edge of the building. I had enough time to scramble up and watch her plummet.

Down, down, down. Red, white, and blue. She screamed most of the way. It took quite a while for her to let go of the cigarette held between her fingers.

"That was wild," I said.

I THINK I'M ALONE NOW

Something in me, deep in my head, agreed. Smiled. Licked its lips.

As far as I could tell, no one had seen me come or go. I left her house by the back door in the kitchen, walked down the narrow alley, passed by the collective light show of ambulance, cop cars, and people gawking.

I stood out front at the bus stop waiting while people bustled around me. Invisible. No one was paying a lick of attention to me and my bookbag. No one cared.

CHAPTER 19

2019 - ST. LUKE'S CHURCH

FATHER O'REILLY STARED AT ME. "We're very glad to have you, Doris. How did you find us?"

"A good friend," I said. "I needed a place of worship closer to home."

"Well, we're always welcoming of a new parishioner. Especially one so excited to participate in the congregation."

"I like to stay busy."

"Youth program, fundraising, our annual Christmas event. You've ticked all the boxes."

I nodded, trying to appear modest. I hated church. Always had. But it was a necessity.

"Has your family always been Catholic?"

I shook my head. "No. I was nothing many years ago. But at fourteen I decided to convert."

A nod.

"Welcome to our family. Let me know if you have any questions."

"I will."

"We like to have a welcome party for our new parishioners.

I THINK I'M ALONE NOW

Would that be okay with you?"

"Absolutely. I'd love that."

A good chance to scope out the faithful flock.

"When's good for you?"

I pulled out my cell phone and consulted my calendar.

CHAPTER 20

1985

NO ONE CAME LOOKING FOR me. No one knew I'd gone home with Karen. And by the end of the following week, I was tight with my two besties again. After the forfeiture of all the money I had stashed away, Melissa forgave me. She had a ton of bright, shiny, current clothes to replace all the stuff I'd destroyed. How could she be mad?

Halloween was swiftly approaching and I think all the mothers wanted us to be back to normal by then.

There had been a brief and exquisite rustle through the school about Karen's suspected suicide, but it had settled pretty fast. Teenagers have bigger things to worry about than the death of one of the herd.

It was Debbie who said, "Who's being what for Halloween?"

I hadn't thought about it. When I thought about anything it was the thing that seemed to want to spoon me while I slept or the whooshing, screaming ride I witnessed as Karen plummeted to the dirty gray city street below.

When I fell asleep, I heard the crunch of her body on impact. Heard the emergency sirens screeching their warning.

I had insomnia, or something like it. When I fell into a fitful slumber, I was often awakened by what felt like phantom arms wrapping around me. Holding me like a lover.

It jerked me awake every time and when I'd pat my shoulder, there would be nothing.

"Go away," I mumbled. That had become my mantra. My protection.

Go away.

"I'm going to be a sexy cat," Melissa immediately piped in.

I did everything in my power not to roll my eyes and still failed.

"What?" she wailed.

"Sexy cat?" I asked.

"Well, yeah. It's a body suit. It *is* sexy."

My fingers picked at a hole in my jeans, worrying the threads until a fresh bit of empty space opened and more of my kneecap appeared.

"Mmmkay," I said.

"Well, what are you going to be?" she challenged.

"I have no idea," I mumbled.

"I think I'll be a witch," Debbie said.

"That's always a good one," Mel said.

I was thinking as they chattered like two little birds. I could be a clown, but that was boring. I could be a hobo, but that was even more boring. I could be one of Charlie's Angels, but that would just be normal clothes.

I'd figure it out later.

"Who wants to go to the mall?" Debbie asked. "My mom said she'd drive us. She needs to find a dress for some work thing. We can hang out while she shops."

I wanted to go to the mall like I wanted another hole in my head, but what was the alternative? Go home, watch TV, doze off due to lack of sleep, get hugged by my own personal monster?

"I'll go," I said.

Off we went again. To the mall.

Oh joy.

I waited while they perused a new shop aimed at girls our age. Nice clothes, knock-offs of the latest trends, but a little more affordable for those of us who didn't have tons of money at our fingertips.

I had even less since I'd forked over all mine to Melissa. Well, not *all* of it. I had about forty bucks in my piggy bank that my mother forgot about.

"It's cute," Debbie said, coming up behind me.

I was stroking a finger absently down the length of the acid-washed denim dress. It was meant to be form-fitting. It had a zipper that ran up the side. The neck was square cut. The sleeves were three-quarter length.

When I stared at it, for some reason, gorgeous MTV video vixens came to mind.

"It's tight," I said.

"How do you know?"

"It's supposed to be." I laughed.

"What's up?" Melissa asked, she had a stack of clothes draped over her arm.

"Dorrie's looking at this dress," Debbie said.

"Cute," Melissa said, shrugging. "Not something you'd normally wear. Little slutty."

I don't know if that was supposed to make me feel bad, but it made me want it more.

When they went to the food court for a big pretzel, I pulled the stowed money out of my purse and paid for the dress. It was small enough that I rolled it up tight and shoved it in my bag with the receipt. No one would know until I wanted them to.

CHAPTER 21

HALLOWEEN EVENING. I WAS TIRED. Very tired. I hadn't slept the previous night. Every time I thought I'd fallen asleep, something stirred me. A whispering, a feathery touch, a jolt, a hand that really wasn't there running down my back.

We were supposed to go trick-or-treating, which I thought was silly. We were fourteen and I was dangerously close to fifteen. A wee bit too old to go out and beg for candy. Especially with Mel dressed as a sexy cat and whatever I was in my acid wash denim dress and heels stolen from my mother. Full face of makeup. Hair done up.

But Alex and Jason were going so Debbie and Melissa were hell-bent on accidentally bumping into them.

I looked so much like my mom getting ready for a date.

Several times while putting on my makeup I stopped and stared at myself, wondering what the hell I was doing.

The answer: I had no idea.

I was just doing it.

They started banging on my door and I ran downstairs to let them in.

"Woah, what are you?" Debbie asked. Her witch costume was

far from sexy. She had a giant wart on the top of her nose and had even put a sprig of hair jutting out.

I laughed.

"I'm a . . . one of Charlie's Angels," I said, because it was the only thing that came to mind.

"Which one. Farrah, right? Definitely Farrah," Melissa said. "Wow. You look *so* much like your mom."

"I know!" Debbie said.

I waved it off. "Let me get a bag or something."

We started off not long after all the porch lights started to pop on.

"After, my mom said she'd make us English Muffin pizzas for dinner. To counteract all the sugar." Debbie rolled her eyes but smiled. "But we have to keep them at the table because last time she made them Dandy ate about six halves and puked all over the kitchen floor."

"At least it was the kitchen floor," I said. "Could have been carpeting."

"True."

We fell in line with lots of other kids, mostly much younger than us. Alex and Jason showed up out of nowhere, turning Debbie and Mel into twittering idiots.

I hung back a little to be free of the cloud of hormones they were all giving off.

Trick-or-treating was boring and uneventful. I was tired and hot, and the dress was like a second skin even in the forty-degree weather.

English muffin pizzas and TV and checking candy was all a blur.

"Dorrie? Are you okay?" Debbie's mother asked. "You look a little pale."

"Tired," I said. "I haven't been sleeping well."

"Oh, that's no fun," she said.

"No shit, Sherlock," was on the tip of my tongue, but I swallowed it down.

"I think I'm going to head home."

I crossed the street, giving Mr. Frank's dark house a side glance. No porch light to welcome kids. No flicker of TV light. No nothing really.

I was wobbly on my heels, unused to walking in them.

In the house, my mother was at the kitchen table.

"You didn't tell me you were going out," she said, her face tight with anger or exhaustion. It was hard to tell.

"Yes, I did. The other day."

"Dorrie, you didn't—"

"I did! It's Halloween! Why *wouldn't* I go out?"

She sighed. "The point is, you didn't say. I was worried."

I glared at her. I had told her. I was sure of it.

I threw my bag of candy on the table and grabbed my cardigan off the back of the chair. Now I was fucking cold.

I slid it on and pulled the hood up over my head.

"And why are you dressed like that?"

I had taken a few steps toward the door. I didn't think she realized. I turned to her. "Like what?"

"Like . . . *that?*"

"What does that mean?" I waited, my hands shoved way into the cardigan pockets. I was furious. I was getting hot again.

"Like a slut," my mother finally said. She spit the word out like a cool smooth stone.

I laughed. At first it was forced, but then it wasn't. I laughed and laughed and laughed until my cheeks ached and my stomach hurt.

"Dorrie!"

My laughter died instantly. "I dressed like a slut because I went as my mother for Halloween," I said.

She was coming at me, most likely to slap my face, when I slipped out the door and banged it shut behind me.

The wind kicked up, the sky was black with churning clouds. They were lit by a moon, hidden behind them somewhere, and the streetlamps.

I stood on the curb, waiting for my mother to come rushing out of the house. Or at the very least, to yell my name and demand I come back.

Instead, nothing happened. The wind whipped, and the sky loomed. The streets were empty, it was too late for the little kids.

Debbie's was my best bet. I'd go there and spend the night and cool off and let my mother do the same.

I walked slowly, dragging my mother's leather high heels along the concrete just to be a bigger asshole. The night was getting colder as I stood there and stared at Debbie's house. I didn't feel like going up there. I didn't feel like explaining.

I was trying to figure out how to go home gracefully. Which was why I didn't hear the noise behind me until his arms were closing around me and the ether-soaked rag was being held over my face and the inside of my head went as black as the Halloween night sky.

PART II

CHAPTER 22

WETNESS. COLDNESS. FIRE. MY EYES flew open and I sat up straight, crying out and sputtering.

Whatever it was rolled down my face, stinging my eyes, my mouth. It was like I'd been doused in rubbing alcohol after running face-first into a thorn bush.

"I didn't know how else to wake you up."

I blinked, hissing, until my eyes cleared enough for me to make out a figure.

"What—"

"I brought you some clothes to change into. It's very cold out tonight and that dress isn't much."

"Mr. . . . Frank?"

He stepped forward and that lit his face a little more. He looked serious, serene, and intent. He always looked a little creepy. He never looked scary.

Right now, he looked scary.

Instead of the fear I anticipated feeling, I felt a rush of bitter rage. I spit out whatever vile liquid had seeped into my mouth.

"Let me go. This is kidnapping."

Mr. Frank nodded. "Indeed, it is. And it's very, very illegal. And yet, here we are."

I spit again and shook my head. "What was that you dumped on me? It stings, and it tastes like shit."

He squatted down in front of me, the overhead basement lights illuminating only half his face. And what appeared to be a large cage. "Does it? Burn?"

"I just said it did."

"What does it taste like?"

"Like when I get hairspray in my mouth by accident. Bitter. Gross. Why? Is this 20 Questions?"

"Huh," he said almost to himself. As if surprised. Then to me: "It's water."

I snorted. "How old is that water? Is it from a swamp?"

"No. Somewhere much different than a swamp. And it's ordinary tap water."

"You better check your tap," I said, squirming.

"There's only one small difference between that water and the water you wash dishes with."

I sighed, feeling a tiny little tingle of trepidation. "If I ask you what it is, will you let me go?"

"No," he said. "But I'll tell you anyway."

I waited, my fingers warring with each other behind my back.

"That water that you're spitting out was blessed by a priest."

"I don't believe in God," I said. As if that had anything at all to do with what he just told me.

"Neither do I," he said, surprising me. I wasn't sure I believed him. "But it doesn't matter if we do. The thing inside of you does," he said.

There was that anger again. A hot flash of it. My cheeks sizzled with heat. I yanked at my restraints, opening my mouth to yell.

Then a wave of vertigo and a rush of fear so intense it stole my breath.

"What thing? What thing, Mr. Frank?" I panted.

He moved a step closer, studying me.

"Dorrie?"

"Yes! You know it's me! You have me tied to a chair in the basement."

"I have *it* tied to a chair," he said with a sigh. "You, dear, are an unfortunate consequence. Have you heard of friendly fire?"

"My brother is a World War II fanatic. I know what friendly fire is."

"You'd be the unfortunate casualty of friendly fire in this scenario, my dear. I want that thing inside you."

"Why?"

"It's evil."

"How did it get there?"

Another sigh. "I'm going to untie your wrists and back out into the outer room and let you put on that sweat suit. It's only getting chillier and your teeth are chattering."

And they were. They were clacking together like the windup teeth my mother put in my Christmas stocking one year because she thought they were funny.

I nodded. "Okay. But you'll come back? And tell me?"

"I will. Are you hungry? There's soup. And cake."

I nodded. I hadn't eaten since lunch. And I was starting to really feel the cold. And the deep dark fear because of what he'd said.

That thing inside you . . .

CHAPTER 23

IT WAS DAMP IN THE basement and I broke out in goose-bumps when I unzipped the dress and stepped out of it.

I kept my back to the door on the off chance he was watching. I didn't think he was. Then again, I was way too freaked out to worry about it.

I folded my dress and dropped a soft over-washed T-shirt over my head, followed by a big sweatshirt. Then I stepped into too big sweatpants and rolled them to cuffs at the ankles. Next, I shoved my frozen feet into huge thick wool socks.

I was still cold. So cold my teeth continued clacking together.

"I'm done!" I yelled.

He came down the steps balancing a tray for me. It held a plastic bowl of soup, a slice of cake on a napkin. Also, a plastic spoon. A Styrofoam cup full of soda and another of water.

"This might help warm you up."

I nodded, accepting the food.

"Are you keeping me, then?" I asked, already knowing the answer.

He let out a mighty sigh and said, "This was all so much easier when Clara was alive. She'd be better at explaining. She'd be better at calming you down."

He drew a milk crate from behind the hot water heater, dragged it into the cage, and turned it over to sit on.

"When that break-in happened, did you feel a lot of . . . stress from it? Anxiety? Did you feel out of control or overly sad?"

My inclination was to lie to him, but my instincts had landed me in his basement with painted windows covered with metal mesh, wearing his or his dead wife's sweats, eating soup with a plastic spoon. Something told me the way I answered this was important.

"I did."

"Did you hide it from everyone?"

I shrugged. "Like you mean, did I keep it to myself?"

He smiled then, reminding me weirdly of Mr. Rogers.

"Yes. That's what I mean."

"My mom works a lot. Like a lot a lot."

He nodded. "I know. A necessity, but still unpleasant."

I swallowed hard. My body was shaking, and I couldn't seem to control it.

He reached down and turned the space heater to a higher setting. The orange glow was somehow more soothing than the heat.

"And Eric, he moved out."

Another nod. "A young man growing up, but still . . . not easy for you, I imagine."

The sudden urge to cry was overwhelming. His kindness was baffling considering I was, for all intents and purposes, a prisoner in his basement. This was something out of a men's adventure magazine. What were his intentions?

I was terrified. But oddly, not of Mr. Frank. I was terrified of *why* he'd decided to bring me here.

"Please tell me!" I blurted. "Why am I here? You seem like a nice, though somewhat creepy, man."

He laughed softly.

"I have a hard time believing you're going to rape me or sell me or worse."

"You're very smart," he said. "But then again, I've always known that."

I waited, holding my breath. I only let it out when I felt dizziness make my head swim.

"I want to help you," he said.

I shook my head but something inside me flexed. It squirmed. A surge of ferocious anger and an aching in my head that made my teeth hurt.

"Do you?"

"I do."

I leaned forward, wondering if I could get to him. Hurt him. If I could do it all before he reacted.

He read my expression because he reached down next to him and picked up a stretch of metal pipe. He sat it across his knees but made no other motion.

"Help me with what, Frank?"

My tongue felt like it was wiggling on its own. My voice had a lilt to it that was unnatural. My cheeks were so warm they felt aflame. Suddenly, I was sweating.

"Your problem."

"And what problem is that?"

"Your visitor."

Another surge of fury and then a nearly equal one of fear. "My period?" I was fucking with him.

"No. You have a hitchhiker in there with you."

All my bones felt molten. The muscles in my cheeks ached, and my mouth opened, and I said, "You're crazy."

But I didn't feel like he was crazy.

"I think something hopped aboard after your encounter with those men. After the shock of it."

I shook my head and tugged the sweatshirt up. I revealed the flat, pale, perfectly taut slice of my underage belly. I wiggled my hips in the seat, knowing that attacking him was out. So, tempting him was my option.

"Come on, Frank. I know you have it in your head. I'm young. You've abducted me." I leaned forward allowing the oversized neck of the sweatshirt to slide off my shoulder. I was braless beneath. My breasts small, perfect, and as yet, untouched.

"She's a—*I'm* a virgin," I said, shaking off my incorrect word choice. "You know you want it. I can read your mind."

He smiled. "I doubt that. If you could read my mind, you'd run."

I sat back, suddenly exhausted. My whole body aching.

"Dorrie?"

"Yeah?"

"Are you in there?"

I snorted. "Where else would I be? You have me trapped."

"It won't be forever, I hope."

That made my blood run cold. "You have to let me out," I snarled.

"Eventually. First, we have to work on making sure you're ready. And you're you."

"And how do we get there?"

"First, you confess."

I lifted my sweatshirt again, even though I'd broken out in a sweat. I hiked it a little higher this time so the underside of my tits were visible.

Frank looked down and away.

"Like what kind of confession?" I pushed. "Forgive me father for I've been a bad, bad girl?"

It's hard to make a sweat suit sexy, but I let my thighs fall wide and hiked my hips forward, so it dragged the worn-in sweatpants tight against my crotch.

"Only you can save me, father. Only you can make me feel better. I've been so terribly bad—"

"Stop it!" he suddenly roared and then I was wet all over again, but it was stinging like acid.

At least he hadn't opted for the pipe.

I shook it off like a dog, screaming the whole time. The acrid smell of burning hair filled my nose and I gagged.

My mind fuzzy, jumping from one thought to the next so fast I couldn't think. I heard myself say, "That's right, you're a church man, aren't you?"

I already knew that. Why would I say that?

"Dorrie! Doris!" His voice was a boom. I felt my eardrums vibrate.

"What!?"

"Listen to me."

I sat there, shaking from the burning wetness.

"Do you know why I spent so much time at church?"

I sighed. "Do I care, old man?"

"You might when I'm done," he said through gritted teeth. "And I'm speaking to Dorrie."

Why did he keep saying that?

"A body can be hijacked in a time of great stress."

Oh, God. Was he a religious nut? Is that why this was happening? I squirmed, rubbing my face over and over. It itched, and it burned.

"You had a time of great stress. It can come for someone who's grieving, who's depressed, who's suffered a trauma or a wound."

My jaw ached. I wanted to scream but held it in.

"They enter, and they sink themselves in and their host may not even notice. I've been watching you since it happened."

"The men?"

"Yes, the men."

"Okaaaaaay."

"I was watching because you didn't have support. Your mother, poor overworked Linda, but she's never home. Eric had moved out. You were left to deal with it on your own for the most part. And you hardly even reacted. I was worried about a demon and it turned out I was right."

I stared at him flabbergasted. Demon? He thought I was possessed by a demon?

I opened my mouth to try and get him to understand he was wrong, and he could let me go. What came out of my mouth was not my voice.

"You fucking nosey worm," I said.

CHAPTER 24

MR. FRANK LAUGHED.

"Anyway, back to me and church. When someone becomes possessed it can go two ways. They know they're possessed, and it terrifies them. Right up to the point where they lose their hold on their own bodies and they go down the rabbit hole. Those people often try to overcorrect. Instead of reaching out to a priest—"

"Worthless pieces of human shit they are," my mouth said.

Mr. Frank paused for a moment and then went on as if I hadn't said a word. "Or if the priest doesn't believe them. Which can happe—"

"Because they're just there for the kiddy diddling," my mouth said.

Terror spiraled through me and I felt my bladder let go. What was happening?

"They attend a lot of church. They might even ask to be rebaptized. Clara and I were active in the church to look for this. I'm a deacon, for what that's worth. But Clara, she practically single-handedly ran the youth program."

"Oh, such a good dead woman. What would make you care so much?"

He'd never tied me back down after letting me change. Big mistake. My body started to rise, fast and smooth, but unexpected. It gave me vertigo.

Mr. Frank pointed the pipe at me and then the spray bottle of water. "Sit. Down. Demon."

My body sat.

I started to cry. Sob. Wailing. But none of it was audible. None of it. I was buried way down deep in my own core and something else was controlling me.

I wanted to go home. I wanted to be warm and safe. I wanted my mother. God, how I wanted my mother. I had wanted my mother for as long as I could remember.

"Why care? We had a daughter . . . die."

I cocked my head. "You petered out there. Die?"

He stared at me.

"Yes, die."

"Of what?"

"Complications."

"Of . . . ?" my mouth said, drawing the word out coyly. Then I laughed.

"None of your business."

There was a very long pause and the sound of rifling inside my head. Like someone running their fingers along paper tabs. Then more laughter leaking out of my mouth.

The part of me down in the hole was surprised. I had never known he'd had a child. It had never really occurred to me.

"Complications of an exorcism," my mouth said. "She was possessed. Poor little Charlotte. Poor little thing. You knew nothing then. Nothing. And the one that got her, boy oh boy, it's a doozie. It must have turned her. Inside. Out."

I licked my lips.

I felt like I was going to throw up. I felt like I had the flu. I was hot, I was cold. My teeth clacked together and sweat ran a line down my back.

Mr. Frank's jaw was so tight I expected to hear his teeth crack.

"Nearly," he said. "But it gave us a goal."

A goal.

"And how will you prove I'm possessed?"

"I think you already have," he said, laughing. "I'd like to help you, Dorrie. Can you hear me?"

Yes! Yes, I can hear you. Help me!

"She can fucking hear you," my mouth said.

"I have a few things I'd like to try. But I doubt they'll work. For tonight, I'll leave you be. Let you rest. I'll bring you a new pair of sweatpants, soap and a washcloth."

He meant because I peed my pants.

I heard myself laughing.

"There's a toilet and a sink behind that partition. If you need it."

"So you can peek? Watch me pee? Are you into that, Frankie? Golden showers? Young girls?"

He stood, taking the piece of pipe with him. He locked the cage behind him. I could see the other parts of the basement, but not get to them. I was like a dog at the pound. I was alone. With it. With whatever was inside me.

CHAPTER 25

EXHAUSTION. HEAVY. FOGGY.

And yet my body roamed, strutted, paced, and shook the cage walls. I clawed at my inner arms, near my wrists. I shook and I swore. Spit flew, and I never did put on those dry sweats.

"Let me out, old man!"

The cage rattled and vibrated. I shook it so very hard I cut my palms. I kept shaking. I ran my bleeding palms down my face and then I followed with my fingernails digging furrows.

My brain was black and red with rage. But part of it was terrified. Confused. Locked in the corner behind the wall of fury, it rocked back and forth and wished for my mother to find me.

Mother. Will she look for me? After what I said, what it said, what we said? Will she find me? Will she care?

"Let me ouuuuuuut," my voice faltered with overuse. I'd been shouting for hours. "I'll suck your cock. I bet it's been a while since good old Clara died, right? Did she do that for you? Or was she a proper thing? Too good for some good old-fashioned dick sucking?"

Silence. Complete, unchanged. Nothingness.

The thing in me exploded with anger. Kicking the cage door so it jumped. Smashing my hands to the wire. At one point I climbed it. I hovered at the top to see if I could get out and when I couldn't, I scaled the chain link ceiling, shaking it like a crazed monkey at the zoo.

Then I fell. My body hit the concrete floor and made a thud that scared me deep down in there under the frenzy. It knocked the wind out of me. It knocked the wind out of it. And there I was suddenly, sobbing and horrible, at the forefront of my own mind.

"Mr. Frank! Mr. Frank! Help me! Help, I fell!" I sobbed uncontrollably and tried to sit up. My entire system was stunned, and I couldn't move.

Had I broken my spine? Was I paralyzed? What was happening?

I heard him at the top of the steps.

"How did you get to the top, Dorrie?"

He didn't explain, but I understood. How was I the one speaking and not my stowaway. "I fell. I fell, and it hurt, and I couldn't breathe and there I was."

"There you were."

A long pause.

"Are you hungry?"

I started to cry harder.

"I'll take that as a yes. I'll get you some food. It's very early in the morning. The sun isn't up yet."

"Okay," I managed.

I still couldn't move or sit up. But I was clear headed and lucid.

Deep inside, I could feel the itch of it in there. The lurker, the shadow, the darkness.

Finally, I rolled to my side and sat up. I could feel my heartbeat in my hip, my butt cheek, my elbow. I pulled my sweatpants down to look at my hip and saw the black and purple bruise rising up.

I put my head in my hands and tried to get myself together.

There were footsteps on the stairs and I looked up to see Mr. Frank with a tray. I smelled toast and eggs.

He slid the tray beneath the fence. There was about a four-inch gap. Then he passed me a small carton of OJ, like they served at school, through the fencing.

I took it with shaking hands. I managed to gulp down about half of it before my hand hurled it at the cage and the orange juice splashed all over Mr. Frank's face.

"Drinks on you!" I howled, laughing.

He sighed.

"Dorrie, if you can hear me, I'm sorry. This thing will abuse you at every turn. It does not care about you because the moment it doesn't need you anymore, it will wreck you, toss you aside, and move on."

I grabbed the cage and pressed my face to the links. "Tell me more, Daddy. Give me a new body. Fresh meat. You pick! I'll inhabit her, and you can do anything. You. Want. Anything! Pick a good one. Maybe one that looks like Clara when she was young. Or that girl you so desperately wanted to bang in college. What was her name? Bernadette? Like the song."

I tipped back onto the cot and started to belt out, "*Bernadette! People are searching for—*"

"That's enough!" he yelled.

"Is it? You wanted her so bad. Little pale redhead who liked to wear green dresses because it set off the color of her locks. She wore those pointy black heels and red lipstick and you used to imagine what that lipstick would look like smeared up the shaft of your cock. What she'd look like if you came in her mouth. If those big blue eyes would grow bigger or if—"

"Doris," Mr. Frank said, very calmly. "I'm going to go upstairs for a bit. Try and eat some if you can. I'll be back in a bit so we can try to talk."

"You wanted to fuck her from behind. Like an animal. And all the while you'd imagine it and jerk off like the pathetic little asshole you were."

He turned on his heels and climbed the steps.

After more ranting and raving, the thing let me eat half a piece of toast and two bites of eggs.

I fell asleep.

I don't know if my body did or not, but I did. And I knew that was a sign I was starting to lose this war.

CHAPTER 26

I DON'T KNOW HOW LONG it took him to come back. I was asleep in the middle of the floor. Not the cot. It looked purplish outside, but I wasn't sure if that was the passage of time or the paint on the windows.

I felt like me but there was no way of telling.

I was humming and when I tried to stop it just kept going. I recognized the tune the way you recognize something you hear in a store on the overhead.

It took me a moment to get it: "Highway to Hell." AC/DC. Not my kind of music, but the thing in me was amusing itself.

To prove that, it started laughing.

"Frank? Frankie?! Your little prisoner is getting hungry again."

I heard his footsteps overhead and saw a few siftings of dust from the rafters here and there. Then the creak of the basement door as he opened it.

He walked down a few steps and then leaned down, so he could see me.

"Spawn of Hell or Dorrie?"

My hands grabbed the band of my sweatshirt and quickly yanked my top up. I shook my torso, so my small breasts bounced, and my mouth cackled: "Who do you think, Daddy?"

Inside my head, I screamed. Screamed so loud my physical throat ached but no sound came out of me. Just the foreign thing piloting my tongue.

"Come give her some food. Or some solace. Flesh and blood can calm the soul. Carnal pleasures are a treasure. . ." It cooed and it laughed and Frank just stood there.

I heard Frank's footsteps recede and my heart sank. Somewhere along the line, he'd become just Frank. I guess when the thing that hijacked your body flashes a guy your tits, you can drop the title of Mister. At least for a while.

I heard him on his way back and hope thrust up inside of me like a plant shoot popping through the spring earth. Hope was a hard thing to find these last few hours.

Footsteps on the old wooden steps.

My head tilted back, and my mouth popped open, and my voice rose. "I'm on the highway to hell!"

Then my breath was gone, I was gasping, lying on my back on the cold concrete floor. My head rang like a bell and I gagged, followed quickly by another gasp for air. Air that wasn't coming.

I groaned and waited for my system to calm.

"Sorry about that, Dorrie," he said softly.

My eyes were weeping from the impact, but I looked up at him in alarm. Had he shot me? He was holding a weapon?

"Bean bag gun," he said with a shrug. "Is that you, Dorrie?"

"Yes," I said.

He seemed dubious.

"I'm sorry you saw my . . . that I shook them—" I gagged and then gasped again. "That wasn't me!" I wailed.

He seemed convinced. He unlocked the cage but brought the bean bag gun with him. He took a seat on the overturned milk crate again and said, "We don't have much time. So, I'm going to explain my plan."

"Can it . . . hear you?"

He sighed. "Probably. But I'm more worried about *you* hearing me and I want you front and center to make sure that's happening. Okay?"

I nodded.

My chest pounded from the blow. My mind whirled. But I was starting to catch my breath and feel better, which meant we had very little time.

"Hurry," I said.

He gave me a succinct nod, stroked the gun, and then said, "I have a plan to try and get it out of you. It's probably not going to be very nice. I will do my best to make it as painless as possible."

"How? How?" I could feel my grip sliding and considered asking him to hit me with the bean bag gun again. But I didn't know if I could take it.

"Sort of like a baptism. But more intense. It was something that worked for Clara and me in the past."

"How many?" I asked. "Over the years. How many have you done?"

"Enough."

"How many have you abducted?"

"Only three. We were usually asked by parents or loved ones. We often were able to do our work in the churches with help and permission from certain clergy."

He sighed and rubbed his eyes before going on. "I don't so much believe in these things. I couldn't really believe in a God that would take my daughter the way she was taken. I lost my faith a long time ago but they're tools, these things I use. The thing inside you, it believes and that's all that matters. I'll use whatever tools I can get."

I nodded, listening intently.

"How many of the priests fucked your wife?" my mouth said.

He sighed. "I'll be back soon, Dorrie. I'm working for you. I'm trying to figure this out. I hope you can hear me."

I wanted to tell him I could, but my body had betrayed me.

"Did you do the priests, too, Frank or don't you swing that way? Was it just Clara, your whore wife?"

I saw it. The flicker of him wanting to shoot me again. Instead, he got the weapon and went to the gate. He unlocked it, checked to make sure he was clear, and then locked it from the other side.

"I'll bring you some food." He stared hard at me. "Let her eat for fuck's sake or your fun will be over very quickly. If you starve her, you're screwed."

"We'll see . . ." the thing said.

CHAPTER 27

THERE WERE DAYS MISSING IN there. They bled into one another. I was aware of very little. I'd come to while clinging to the roof of the cage or beating the window wire with my hands. Screaming. Peeing my pants. Hurling food.

And every time it would push me back down, hold me under, take me out of the picture.

My clothes and hair were filthy. I'd lost weight. I smelled like body odor and feces and slowly rotting flesh.

I came to during daylight hours with bloody fingernails and knuckles and my face being bathed in sun and crisp fall air.

I gasped.

I was hanging there from the small basement window. I'd managed to peel the wire mesh covering off to get to the glass. Then I'd busted the glass. With my fist, it appeared. I had glass slivers in my palm and beneath my shredded nails from the window.

Cold fall wind blew over my face and felt sweet. Like freedom. But I was also panicking. If I had my head sticking out the window, then the thing in me had its head sticking out the window.

A deep woof came to me and I let out a strangled cry.

Dandy! It was Debbie's big dumb dog.

"Dandy!" I yelled. My voice was some withered thing. Raspy and sickening. Then it curled with maliciousness.

"Daaaaaaaandeeeeeeee!" I whistled.

I can't whistle. Had never been able to master it no matter how much I tried.

Another woof and then the rattle and jingle of his collar.

I could feel him pounding toward me.

Then there he was, all 110 pounds of Saint Bernard and slobber. He was licking me, licking me joyously.

"Good boy," I said. "Good, good boy."

My hands shoved into his thick pelt, I grabbed his collar, and yanked him toward me. Two purposes, to help me up some and for the hell of it.

He bowed, swayed, and when I yanked again it drove his thick neck against the ragged shards of window glass.

A yelp so loud and so sharp it hurt my ears. He was bleeding but still panicking and fighting it. I yanked again, driving his neck down again.

A howl this time.

I was on borrowed time. If Frank heard, he'd come down. This was unusual. This wasn't the ranting and raving of a trapped possessed girl. This was a fight to the death between monster and beast.

I yanked again and this time he barked and then went limp. Dandy twitched and whimpered but the blood was rushing hot and thick over my hands.

And then it paid off.

"Dandy? Dandy!?"

Debbie's voice.

I heard Frank's footsteps on the floor overhead. Heard him start to run when I shouted.

"Help! Help! Debbie help! Help me! I'm here! Down here!"

There was a pause and then her voice, high and frightened, "Hello? Dandy? Dandy, where are you?"

I yelled again and was rewarded with her voice. Confused, winded, and hurrying my way.

"Hello? Dorrie! Is that you?"

"Help me," I howled.

Frank was running down the steps. His feet beating out a tattoo on the wooden risers. The keys jingled as he hurriedly tried to get them out of his pocket.

"He's got me! Frank—Mr. Frank! He's got me! Help me, Debbie!"

Debbie rounded the corner of the house and her eyes flew wide. So wide it would have been comical were I not hanging there in the busted window, bloody and smelling like mildew and shit. "Dorrie! Dandy!"

She grabbed ahold of her behemoth of a dog and tugged. Dandy rallied. He wiggled and bucked, blood still rushing from his thick neck.

The thing in me was sad to see the big lug hadn't died. The small part of me that soldiered on was filled with relief. So much that I sobbed aloud.

"Dorrie! Oh, my God! Where have you been?" she said it as she dragged Dandy away. Then she hurried back.

The gate behind me swung open and I yelped. "Help! Hurry!"

"Have you been there all this time? Your mother is—"

I didn't hear the rest because something hit me in the back. Then it happened again. It felt like he was pelting me with bricks, but I was willing to wager that I'd just suffered some hits from the bean bag gun.

"Dorrie! Dorrie!" I could still hear Debbie screaming. Then her face appeared in the broken window. She tried to shield her eyes and see inside but Frank was dragging me into the depths of the basement, toward the steps.

"Right. I guess we're stepping this up, demon. I was trying to keep the plan intact. But one has to be adaptable. It's what keeps us alive."

"She's going to call the cops on you," I railed. "They're going to find you and charge you as the fucking pedophile you are. Kiddie diddler! Abductor! Monster! Molester!"

My feet beat against every step as he muscled me up the staircase. My back bowed, and I hissed like I'd been burned.

He was chanting. Latin words that flowed from him and made no sense to me but irritated the thing hijacking my body.

I kicked and bit and then something hit me on the temple, hard, and the world grayed out.

CHAPTER 28

2019

I'D MANAGED THE WELCOME PARTY of parishioners and their families without feeling too much like the odd man out. The falsity of it was hard. Being around people who viewed themselves as a community while living a constant solitary lifestyle was a struggle, but it had a purpose. I paid close attention. Took mental notes. And a few weeks later, when I was invited by one of the youth ministers to help with the kids, I went eagerly.

That was probably going to be my best bet to find anyone who might need my help. It wasn't always the case, but it was often a success.

It was our first youth night.

We were making Christmas nativity ornaments. I'd have gone for Santa, but that's just me.

I watched them all as I walked around. Children are easy. Children are often distraught and open and completely innocent.

They suffer at the hands of adults, of one another, of society. They are overlooked, forgotten, abused, and neglected.

They're prime pickings.

They are wounds waiting to happen.

I watched Daniel. Possibly named by his parents for the tale of

Daniel and the Lion. Who fucking knows?

My eyes, though, kept going to Kaley. Her face was a bit dirty, her hair askew. She'd been dropped off a half hour before the program started and I would wager she'd be the last here and I'd have to wait with her.

Her father, who didn't seem particularly interested in what she'd be doing or in the church's activities, had rolled through as if he'd dropped her off a thousand times. Which he probably had. I'd say this was a free babysitting scenario.

Which meant Kaley was probably passed to whoever would watch her at any given time.

She looked up at me and smiled.

Was that smile as curled and wicked as it looked to me, or was I being too sensitive?

"Nice work, Jake," I said, and patted the little boy's red hair.

"Very good, Marcy." I was phoning it in now. Watching Kaley as she worked.

She looked up at me again and blinked. Green eyes flashed to black eyes flashed to green eyes.

It's your imagination, Doris. It's flashbacks. PTSD. Fear. Whatever you want to—

"Stare much?" she said softly as I got closer.

Brave. Flippant. Knowing?

"What's this?" I asked, trying to keep my voice level.

"The baby Jesus," she sing-songed.

Baby Jesus was a mangled lump of flesh and his eyes were black holes. She'd written her name with almost machinelike precision and her cradle was impeccable. She wasn't sloppy or less artistic than her fellow attendees. The appearance of the baby was deliberate.

"Are you sure?"

"Of course, I'm sure," she snickered.

The sound sent a trickle of cold up my spine.

I looked at the clock. "Time to pack up kids. Your parents should be here soon."

I'd be keeping an eye on Kaley.

CHAPTER 29

1985

I WAS IN THE TRUNK. The car was gliding. It was a big Chevrolet Malibu, gray with maroon interior. I'd seen him arrive home from work in it enough times to know.

I was in the trunk, but I could still hear the radio playing. Classical music. Of course.

"Mr. Frank? Let me out!" I kicked the trunk.

The music cut out and he said, "Dorrie?"

"Yes. I'm awake. Let me out. I can't breathe. I'm scared."

It smelled like gas, oil, old leaves, and cold air in the trunk. I felt around but all I could find was a snow scraper, a blanket, a bottle of motor oil, and a jack. The jack was under me and, I was pretty sure, ridiculously heavy.

"Doris, I'm sorry it's going like this."

I was going to correct him for calling me Doris and then I thought better of it. I was tired. The stench in the trunk of my own body was overwhelming. Something was inside me. I had killed—or nearly killed—Dandy. A big stupid dog, but one I loved. And now I was being taken to a new location in the trunk of a car.

My teeth chattered, and I tried to cover myself in the old wool blanket. It made my nose itch.

"This thing, even if I can get rid of it, will cause a scar. A scar that can rip open at any time in the future."

I was listening, holding my breath. "A scar?"

"Yes. And it's an easy access point. The thing in you might leave—I hope to get it to leave—but it can leave an opening for something in the future. Something lesser . . ."

"Or something worse," I said under my breath.

But apparently, he heard me, even above the sing of the tires on the road and the engine, he heard me. "Yes."

We came to a stop and my feet started pounding the trunk. My fists followed suit. I was terrified and thinking but the thing in me was pitching a fit.

"Help! Help! This man stole me! He abducted me. He—"

The trunk popped open and gray autumn light flooded the trunk. I threw up my arm and a wave of nausea overcame me.

"You can scream all you want," Mr. Frank said. "We're out by the reservoir. There's no one here. It's early November, it's drizzling, it's cold, and there's nothing to do here. Plus, we're behind the marked-off perimeter. Scream your head off, monster."

I stared at him. By the reservoir? There were a ton of woods out there. Rivers, waterfalls, rocks, cliffs in places.

What was he going to do? Kill me?

"I'll suck your dick," my mouth said. "Just don't kill me."

His jaw grew tense, his eyes dark. He shook his head.

"Don't worry, Dorrie. I know that wasn't you. And I'm not going to kill you."

His mouth said he wouldn't hurt me, but his eyes said he *hoped* not to hurt me. But we'd see.

Mr. Frank reached into the trunk and brushed the blanket aside. He grabbed my shirt front and hiked me up. My hair swung in my face—greasy, smelly, tangled.

I was a hag version of myself. The thing in me didn't care about the shell.

He helped me out of the trunk and I stumbled.

"Where are we going?" I snapped.

"For a walk," Frank said.

He held the back of my tee and hustled me down a worn path.

"Why are we back here? We shouldn't be back here. It's restricted." I was babbling.

"I come back here once in a while. Clara and I used to come

here. We'd walk and talk and remember our girl, Charlotte."

I gagged. I felt very sick. A rebellion from my internal visitor or the car ride in the trunk?

Frank had a bag slung over his shoulder.

"How did your daughter end up like me?" It was my question and my voice. Which surprised me.

"There was a boy. At school. He . . . hurt her," Frank said softly.

"Ah, the good old rape scenario," my mouth said.

I felt my cheeks flush from frustration.

Frank didn't react. He just kept marching forward. "She had a hard time afterward," he went on. "She became very withdrawn. Kept to herself. She'd always been a quiet girl but this took it to an entirely different level. She slept a lot. Suffered nightmares, anxiety, acting out. And then one day . . ." He let it go. Right there.

I tripped on a root, went down on my knees. Cold water from recent rain soaked through my stained sweatpants. I looked down into the puddle. My face stared back at me. But not my face. Something off about it. Twisted. Sad. Dark.

Ruined.

He helped me up and we kept walking. The mud sucked my shoes off and I was suddenly barefoot. My feet were freezing. He paused and let me shove my muddy feet back into my sneakers.

My teeth chattered, sounding almost comical. My head swam and the world faded at the edges.

"We're almost there," he said.

I nodded.

"And then one day?"

"What?" he asked.

"You said she was having a real bad time and then one day."

He looked up at the aluminum-gray sky. "Then one day it escalated. Her anger was over the top. She hurt our—we used to have a small dog," he said. "Then a neighbor girl. Then a neighbor boy. She pushed him out— "

He stopped but I pushed.

"She pushed him out of a what?"

"Not out of. Out into. She pushed him out into the street in front of a moving car. He died. And Clara thought she'd seen something wrong with Charlotte's eyes right after it happened. Something shift in her face. Something we couldn't understand. It was Clara who put two and two together."

"And you think that because some men broke into my house, robbed us, and terrorized me, I'm like your daughter?"

"No," he said, prodding me again. "I think, because all that happened and you had virtually no one to turn to, you felt very alone and scared. Your sadness grew and went unnoticed and still you had no one. That's why."

I sighed. I was very tired. My bones ached. My head throbbed.

We rounded the bend in the road. My sneakers were coated in muck and so were his nice winter boots. The cuffs of his pants were stained with it. The bottom of my sweatpants had wicked up water. I shivered and shook and tasted metal in my mouth.

"Please . . ." I said when the water came into view. A shallow rocky river. Just deep enough to drown someone.

"Be brave, Dorrie," he said.

I sobbed. The panic was very real. Yes, there was something in me. I knew that. I accepted it. But, at the moment, it was letting me drive. I was front and center and very aware I was being led to my death, no doubt.

And he was justified, I knew.

"They'll come looking for me," he said. "Soon. That's why I had to take you. Debbie saw you so she'll no doubt call the police. As she should of course," he said softly.

He patted his pocket as if assuring himself whatever he thought was there was actually there.

"Mr. Frank. You don't need to—"

"It will be okay. It will all work out."

"Did you tell your daughter that when you killed her?"

"Yes," he said.

I shut up then.

CHAPTER 30

WE WERE AT A PART of the creek where the water moved slower. The water looked nearly still unless you stared at it hard. There was possibly a nearby beaver that was to thank.

"Are you going to drown me?"

"I'm going to try to save you," he said. He patted his pocket again.

"What's in there? A gun?"

He laughed. And honest to god real laugh. "Not even close. I'm hoping that my wife and my daughter can help me with getting you back to your old self. There are tools beyond those born of Christian mythos. Very personal ones. But I need you to remember, in case anything happens, that scar will be there. That scar will never leave. It's like a beacon. An opening. It might as well be a neon sign to disembodied things looking for a warm place to curl up and take root."

My stomach heaved, and I threw up all down the front of myself.

"It's okay. You'll be clean soon enough."

"What if something does happen to you? What will happen?" I wished, in a weird way, that the thing in me would take front and center. This felt too big. Too real. Too much.

"I don't know. At the very least I'll go to jail for a while. Taking a girl and holding her hostage in my basement is not legal by any extent."

"But I'm-I'm sick," I stammered. "I'll explain. I'll help."

It was dawning on me as we walked, me covered in mud, rain, and puke, that if something happened to Mr. Frank, he was the only person who really knew what was going on with me. I would be in a very bad position.

I would possibly be hijacked by this thing forever.

I would never be me again.

He pushed me down onto a rock, so I was seated. Then he sighed. It was possibly the most exhausted sound I'd ever heard. "Dorrie, there is very little chance that I, even with your help, could convince anyone of what's actually going on. It's going to be cut and dried to cops. One look around my basement will confirm whatever Debbie tells them."

"You could take me. You could take me, and we could run, and you could help me."

He cocked his head.

"Dorrie? Why so worried about me?"

Tears started to run down my face. I was leaking. And not in a supernatural way. Just a normal fourteen-year-old girl way.

"Because you care," I mumbled.

"What?" He squatted in front of me and both his knees cracked like small gunshots. I giggled with nerves at the sound.

"Because you care!" I said more vehemently. "Because you noticed. Because you wanted to help me. Because you showed up when I needed someone. And that's not what I'm used to in my life."

He looked like he was going to cry and that made me cry harder.

"It will be okay," he lied.

He held his hand out. "Do I have to fight you?"

I answered honestly. "Not yet."

I took his hand and stood. We walked hand in hand to the water's edge. In another life, with another couple, it could have been a date or a marriage ceremony. In our case, it was the end of something. Either the thing in me or the me left in me.

"It will be okay," he said again.

CHAPTER 31

2019

"THAT'S A NICE COLORING JOB, Kaley," I said. It wasn't. I was lying. Her picture of the holy family was colored all in black and shit brown. She dragged the crayons across the paper like she was trying to drive it through.

As usual, the heat was cranked because it was winter. It was cranked too high. I was sweating.

I took off my cardigan and draped it over the back of the desk chair.

Our evening was about to come to an end. We had to finish coloring pages, listen to a parable, eat a snack, and pick our names for Secret Santa.

I was the one who had pushed for Santa. They'd balked at first but no one wants to lose the woman who offers free help all the time.

So far, the evening youth group had been okay.

But I was still watching Kaley carefully.

I dropped my phone by accident and bent to get it.

"That's a mighty nasty arm, sis. What happened to you? Something get ahold of you? Something get after you?"

Kaley. She said it in a sly voice. Amused. Snickering.

"An accident," I said. "When I wasn't much older than you."

"You know the ways of the world then," she said with the mouth of a much older person. "You know the world is a festering pile of shit."

I looked up at her suddenly. Her eyes shifting, flicking, like nictating lenses in a predator.

"Hi there, sis. I might as well cop to being here. Because there's not a damn thing you can do about me. You can't help this kid."

"Maybe you're right," I said.

Then another youth night guide showed up in the doorway.

"But I can sure as hell try," I said under my breath as I went to talk to her.

I looked back at Kaley from the doorway. Her head was down in her hands and she appeared to be sleeping.

I hoped, trapped in there with that thing, the original soul was okay.

CHAPTER 32

1985

THE MOMENT I HIT THE cold creek water my body revolted. I went rigid and heard the strangest sound. I realized it was me. Hissing at him.

"You could make it easy and just leave her," Mr. Frank said.

"You'd like that," I growled.

"Actually, yes, I would. Just think. If you leave, we're done. No messy battle and all that."

My leg swung out and kicked Frank right above the kneecap. His face went pale and his body went down. I didn't see him put his hand in his pocket.

I started to run but his arm reached out, snagged my ankle, and pulled me down. I went face-first into the frigid water, my teeth smacking together hard enough that I tasted blood. I felt the grit of a sliver of tooth on my tongue as I tried to scramble to my feet. I slipped on the smooth river rocks.

When I looked up he'd managed to get the lid off the bottle he'd plucked from the bag he'd carried. The bag now floated off like a deflated sea creature. The water from the bottle hit me in the face and I laughed.

Until fire filled my eyes and mouth. Until my skin sizzled and I smelled my own burning hair. Holy water. But not just any holy water. Something more. Something added to the old boring Christian standby.

I was screaming but still managed to pick out his words as he caught his breath, huffing. "My wife had a bunch of water blessed when she was still alive. She had a friend from grade school who knew a monsignor. The monsignor had access to the Pope. The Pope is like any other man. He does favors."

I hit him and he went down on one knee but recovered. "Clara was the one who believed. That's what this water is. Her belief. The love of my life's faith. Her commitment. It's selfless love in a bottle."

I pawed at my face, clawing at my skin, feeling skin slough off as I did so. The screams coming out of me were drawing blood. I could feel the sting of it in my throat.

I dropped to my knees.

He stooped over, hands on knees, catching his breath. Frank was not a young man. He wasn't exactly old, but he surely wasn't a teenager.

I winged a rock at him. Almost blindly. My eyes were swollen, and they wept from the fire of the Holy Spirit. Usually just uncomfortable, but this also contained the love of a dead woman who tried to save her daughter.

"Fuck you," I managed and then vomited into the slowly moving river.

He chuckled.

I reached out and grabbed his ankle, following his lead. I yanked him, and he went down on his ass in the water. The splash hit my face and relieved some of the pain. The water was cold and clear and felt like heaven. Pun intended.

Frank was scrambling with his hands, patting his pockets, water dripping from his face and hair.

"Help me, Clara," he muttered. "Help me, Charlotte."

I laughed, snorting water up my nose by accident. Scorching my sinuses and down the back of my throat.

"They can't fucking help you. They're dead. As dead as you're about to be. Do you believe in Hell? You should. Because you're going to go there. You abducted a young girl," I gasped. Everything still burned. Pain rolled across my skin. Filled my head.

The Pope, who knew?

"Help me, Charlotte!" he called out to his dead daughter. Taken long ago by a thing like the one in me.

Then something hit me in the face. It felt like sand and tobacco and it stuck to me. Coating me. Filling me with stunning heat and crippling dread. Suddenly. Totally. It filled my mouth and stuck in my eyes.

He dropped what he was holding. A small vessel for cremains.

He'd flung some of his dead daughter's ashes at me.

What kind of faith, hope, and love were those magical bits infused with? How much pain and hope and effort did they encapsulate?

My skin felt like the sun. The water around me boiled, rubbing against me, burning me more. Every lick of the river water was agony.

This was far worse than any holy water. Far worse than a sprinkling from God's own water fountain. This was a lifetime of love and the unadulterated sorrow of loss.

I pulled at my arms instinctively and a slim sheet of skin came off.

In the background, Mr. Frank was mumbling. Words I couldn't understand but the thing inside me certainly recognized. I heard his wife's name again, his daughter's, and felt very sure he was channeling those lost to him. Their love and their power.

I hit the water ass first. The rocks banged against my tailbone and I shivered from the impact. But then my brain remembered my severe pain and I backpedaled away from him.

"Not you! No. You are useless. You are not a threat to us! You are not what will end us."

My ass was raw, my clothes soaked and heavy, and I was smoking. Gagging on the smell of my own burned flesh. It itched and burned and ached all at once. The places where the cremains stuck smoked and blackened, like a hot dog over a campfire.

He reached for me, snagged my wrist in a tight grip and hauled me toward him. His pleas to the ether louder. His words more painful. The look in his eyes the look of a man who would not stop. Would not surrender.

I felt around with my hand. Small rocks, trash, silt all sifted through my fingers as he yanked me up.

"My daughter did not die in vain! My wife either! I will help Dorrie. *Someone* has to help Dorrie!" he roared.

My hand closed around a lump and I snagged it. I brought it up in a wide arc and missed. It thumped against the top of his shoulder and he let out a pained "Oof!"

But he was pretty much unharmed.

"No! Nonono!" I flailed again, pulled back against him. Once more I missed. I dropped the rock and it splashed far on the other side of him.

Somewhere overhead a plane buzzed in the gray sky. Could they see us? What appeared to be a fourteen-year-old gangly girl fighting with a middle-aged man in the middle of a stream?

Or did they see us for what we really were? Something evil, someone good. The classic battle. Devil versus angel.

Hot fresh pain flooded my arm. The arm he held. Had he cut me? Hit me?

No, I realized, as I watched. My arm was sloughing the top layer of skin. As he held me and as I pulled, my skin was sliding down like a fancy evening glove. The burns so bad I'd become raw flesh in a too-big bag.

"No!" he growled, trying to get a better grip. Trying to grab me with more force.

I fell on my ass as he continued to hold the flesh of my hand and wrist and forearm. Only now it was empty. A flesh condom.

I giggled.

He started toward me as my hands scrabbled in the freezing cold water. I grabbed the first thing I could get a tight grip on, swung wildly, the thing in me hissing even though I could tell—could *feel*—it was terrified on a level it had never experienced. Frank was a true adversary. This was survival of the fittest. This was a battle to the death.

Frank hit me hard, driving me back into deeper water. His hands found my throat. Squeezing. Squeezing so hard tiny fairy lights ignited in my field of narrowing vision. I tried to gasp for air, failed. I found a mouthful of water instead.

I sputtered and choked. The edges of what vision I had left were fading out. My mind was narrowing down to a dark point in the nothingness.

I gagged and used my legs for leverage. Kicking and thrashing as his fingers, somehow so thick and so strong despite the cold and his age, slowly squeezed the reality away from me.

Was I about to die? Was the thing inside me dying? What was

happening?

Another gasp and another gulp of water. This time water from his bottle was mixed in. I knew because my throat started to burn and bubble. I tasted blood. I tasted metal, I tasted ash and burnt bones and death.

"Die," he said. "Not you Dorrie. You hang on. You stay with me. I want to bring you back. I want you to be okay. I want you to know you are loved and you are valuable. We need you here. The world needs you here."

My throat felt tight but this time due to emotion. How to help him help me? Just lie here and die?

Inside me, something blinked its eyes, found its reserve, and acted.

The thud traveled up my arm, jolting my shoulder harshly. Making something pop in that joint and causing a twinge of pain. I felt the impact jar me. Saw the rock strike his temple. Watched the light almost instantly fade from his eyes and his head tilt to the side. His shoulders slumped forward, body went soft, and down into the water he slithered.

Next to him floated the skin of my arm.

Just then a limb fell from the tree overhead. I saw it coming but not soon enough to move out of the way. It hit me full speed in the face, rocking me back into the water against the river stones.

The world exploded with a white flash and then faded out to gray static.

I sank.

CHAPTER 33

2019

"I'LL TELL THEM YOU'RE MESSING with me," she said. "You know, touching me and stuff."

I blinked and felt my insides turn heavy. How much did that remind me of me talking to Frank? How much did that wrench my heart?

"Why is that?"

"I know what you're doing," she said. This was no normal nine-year-old. Nope.

"What's that?"

"Grooming me," she said.

I laughed. Was I possibly wrong? Was she simply a precocious kid who had seen too many shitty adults?

I sighed, grabbed two bottles of water from the church's basement fridge.

We were waiting for her father. Or her mother. If either of them bothered to show up with their glassy eyes, too thin limbs, and constant scratching. Her mother would pick at scabs on her arms while waiting to drop Kaley off.

"I'm actually just waiting with you until a guardian shows up," I lied. "Do you have grandparents?"

She shrugged. Her stare was that of a very old woman who'd seen a hard life, not a kid.

"Yeah. But only one and she's in Florida. I see her once or twice a year. Once when I was little, I went down there for a week. I got to swim in the ocean and eat food sold out of huts on the beach."

Another flicker of empathy sounded inside me. Was she? Was she just a regular kid?

"When I came home was the first time they pimped me out. They'd run out of Oxy while I was gone."

I blinked. She said it casually. I had been lulled. Lulled into believing the only thing inside her was the soul of a little girl.

I sat at the table, set the water bottles on the floor.

"When they realized it worked, they did it as often as they could. Sometimes, I'd know, and I'd take off. Still do. One day, I'll get fed up and gut them while they sleep."

There was the wound. The scar. The betrayal and neglect.

My heart hurt. For the little girl. Not the hitchhiker.

She gave me the side eye. "She's safer with me in here, you know."

I reached into my pocket and fingered the item stashed there.

"Why is that?"

"I'll keep her safe."

"You'll end up putting her in jail."

She shrugged, looking ancient and feral in that moment.

"Beats being pinned beneath some big sweaty middle-aged guy who just bought himself an hour with you from your parents."

I'd turn them in. It was that simple, I tried to fool myself.

I'd come to this church for this reason. But first I had to make sure I was right.

I opened my bottle of water. The one I'd swapped out. I got the lid off and "accidentally" knocked it over. It sprayed everywhere, splashed, pooled and ran. All over her.

One of Frank's practical tools. Nothing more.

The moment it touched her, Kaley jumped up, hissing. Skin burning.

She screamed at me. Lunged at me. I backpedaled and aimed the water bottle with its remaining contents at her.

We stood there. Squaring off.

"Hi," I said. "I once was just like you, Kaley. I once had an unwanted hitchhiker."

I THINK I'M ALONE NOW

The outer doors opened and we both froze.
Her parents were here to get her. Or one of them was.
I'd let her go. For tonight.

CHAPTER 34

1985

I TURNED ON MY SIDE and puked. My face had been fully submerged in water. The torrential rain had pelted my face until it filled my nose and throat. When I rolled into the river, it sealed the deal.

I sat straight up, the pain in my arm almost sending me back down. It was cold, and the water was freezing. It had kept the pain somewhat at bay. When I sat up out of the river—gasping for air, head aching, confused—the exposed skin sang with agony.

I sobbed.

Then I remembered.

Shivering, I got on hands and knees and searched the river.

It was raining hard. The water was deeper.

"Mr. Frank?"

My memory was better than I'd have liked. I remembered the shoulder-jarring thud of the rock in my hand connecting with his temple. The sick wet meat sound of the impact. The light fading from his dark brown eyes. The way he'd slumped.

I'd killed him.

I'd killed Mr. Frank.

The thing inside me was to blame. But no one but me and Frank knew that, and he was dead.

I saw his boot first. A slick, shiny object pointing toward the sky. I staggered my way over there and dropped to my knees by his body. His eyes were already milky, staring straight up at nothing. His hand curled against his pocket as if still seeking.

"Mr. Frank?" My voice was so soft. Painfully soft over the roar of the river. I shook him.

His head lolled, and his eyes stared at me, accusing and milk glass bluish white.

I ran my hands through my hair. Feeling every ache and pain. My empty stomach. My shredded fingertips and my mangled feet and the crust of dandruff in my hair.

Was I alone in here?

I started at him again and followed the arc of his now stiff hand to this pocket. Shoving my hand past his and into the recesses, my fingers closed around a small bottle and pulled it out. Glass. Maybe a maple syrup bottle?

It was full of water. But I knew it wasn't just any water. It was holy water.

I acted on instinct. I dribbled some on his forehead and hesitantly put my finger in it and made the sign of the cross.

I knew he didn't believe in God or heaven so much as his work, but he deserved the effort. Even if it was from someone who didn't believe in it either.

I waited. Waited for the jolt of pain from touching it. From making the sign of God and all that was holy on his skin.

Nothing.

A wave of giddiness swept over me. I sat back on my haunches, dizzy and suddenly utterly exhausted. If I tipped over in the water, I was afraid I'd stay there and not move. Too defeated and beleaguered to go on.

I tilted the bottle back and sipped it slowly.

Nothing.

I took a bigger gulp, realizing then how fucking thirsty I was.

Nothing.

I guzzled the whole thing, and nothing happened.

I looked down at him. "You did it," I said. "I think I'm alone now."

I put my head down on his chest and cried until I felt like I'd been hollowed out.

It was then that I heard a sharp whistle and raised my head.

A woman waved at me from the bank of the creek. She had a yellow lab on a leash. It was straining to get to me, but she was holding it back.

"Is everything okay?" she shouted. "Are you alright? Do you need help?"

I waved back. "Help!" I yelled. "Help me!"

Then I sat and waited.

~

The police picked me up out of the river. It was like the slow-motion ending of a movie about a predator and its prey. The only problem was, Mr. Frank hadn't been a predator, but there was no way to explain that. And no one would believe me.

I settled for repeatedly reassuring the cops that I was okay.

They rushed me to the hospital due to the arm. The injury was severe, the treatment painful, and the pain followed me into adulthood from the scarring.

But I was alive.

"He didn't . . . did he hurt you? In . . . that way?" My mother was struggling to ask me if I'd been raped. My brother stood nearby, his mouth a thin line.

He'd moved back in while they were looking for me.

"No. He didn't. I don't . . . I don't know why he took me," I lied. "But he didn't hurt me. Not like that, not in any way."

"His basement has a giant cage," Eric said through a clenched jaw. "And you were in that cage, Dorrie. He hurt you."

"He kept me. He didn't hurt me," I said. My voice was faraway, my brain very tired.

"What's it called?" my mother mumbled to him. "Stockholm Syndrome?"

He nodded subtly.

I was too tired to argue. The cops brought me a hot chocolate in a Styrofoam cop and one of them draped me in a BCPD coat.

"Can I go home?" I asked.

"Soon," he lied.

Instead, we were all taken to the precinct where I told my story over and over again.

I never wavered. My words never changed.

I learned that Dandy was okay, and my face had been plastered all over the news and billboards.

I THINK I'M ALONE NOW

I put my head down at some point as my mother spoke to the police. I fell asleep that way. I could smell my own breath, my own hair, and the disinfectant, institutional smell of the precinct.

None of that mattered. I listened to the drone of my mother, brother, and the police officers. I listened to the silence inside me.

I was the only one in there.

But I hadn't forgotten about the scar.

CHAPTER 35

MIDDLE-AGED MAN ACCUSED OF abducting fourteen-year-old girl dies in accident. Frank Brinks, 52, was found dead in an offshoot of the High Hill River in High Hill, Maryland last Tuesday afternoon. Blunt force trauma was the cause of death according to the ME. He was killed by Doris "Dorrie" Travis, 14, of Baltimore. She was his captive for over a week, having been taken the night of Halloween. She was held in his basement for the duration of her time missing. Ironically, Doris's family lives directly across the street from the accused.

Her friend, Deborah Millstone, the next-door neighbor to Brinks, alerted the police after her dog was harmed while it was trying to save Doris by pulling her from the basement window.

The dog was treated for its injuries and is doing well.

Doris was taken to the hospital and given care before talking extensively with the police about her abduction.

Frank Brinks is survived only by distant family. His wife, Clara, died in 1982 from cancer and his daughter in 1976 from an accident.

I THINK I'M ALONE NOW

Details are still emerging as the police continue to interview Doris and her family.

~

My mother put the paper down and eyed me up. "Did you get enough to eat?"

I nodded.

I hadn't eaten anything but a strip of bacon and a sip of juice, but that's all I cared to eat. The anxiety I was experiencing was extreme. I thought I'd be relieved. I thought I'd relax. But all I could think of was that scar he'd told me about.

After the trauma of killing him, wasn't I simply an open door to whatever else wanted to come along? Drag itself from hell, hitch a ride on a spirit conjured by kids playing with Ouija boards, or slither its way into existence at the scene of violence or pain or crime.

I swallowed hard.

"The police said there's someone you can talk to you if you're having some trouble."

I looked at her expectantly.

"A therapist. They have them there for kids—well, not just kids—people in general who went through things like you did. Do you think you'd like to talk to someone?"

She said it all nonchalantly as if trying to approach a shy, scared horse.

I nodded. "Yes," I blurted, surprising her.

If I didn't deal with this, I'd be a waiting home for something bad. I'd be putting out a welcome mat.

I didn't want that. I couldn't think of a worse thing.

I went to therapy.

I went to church because I knew he was right. It was a tool regardless of my own disbelief.

I watched. I waited. I listened. I felt.

I broke into Frank's house one day when the neighborhood was quiet, and I found his diary and that of his wife, Clara.

I read. I studied. I found her cremains and some that were labeled Charlotte. I hoped they might keep me safe. There was no one to know they were missing, so they came home with me in my pockets. I stored Clara in a tea tin and Charlotte in an old glass bottle.

Things became normal again. Until one day when I was about twenty, I saw a kid. A kid like me who had something hitching a ride inside them.

That kid was a hard case, but I managed to help her. I like to think I had the spirits of Frank, Clara, and Charlotte by my side and not just bits of ash and bone.

I began to visit church regularly as more than a parishioner. I was hunting. I was picking up where Frank had left off.

To this day I remember that scar inside me. I guard it vigilantly. Always aware that it's an entry to my soul.

CHAPTER 36

2019

SHE PUSHED HIM DOWN INTO the stairwell. I saw it happen and then I heard the wail of that poor boy.

She turned to me, dark eyes flashing, a smile that seemed to have too many teeth spread across her face.

My stomach rolled. How long before a kid was tossed off a roof or a kitten was killed or worse?

Kaley.

I ran over, the other children clustering. Poor Gabe, lying at the bottom of the steps that led to the church basement, one leg pointing in the wrong direction. But he was caterwauling, which was a good sign.

"Kaley did it," Stephen said. "I saw her push him. Then she ran out."

I looked up to find her gone. I called 911 from my cell and called over to the other Sunday school teacher.

"Can you stay here? With them? I need to see if I can find Kaley."

Kaley was by the woods on the edge of the parking lot poking a dead bird with a stick.

"My kind could have entered this bird and woken it up once upon a time. Now we need living vessels."

The hair on the back of my neck stood on end. I fingered the small vial in my pocket.

A frat boy's best friend in a crowded bar. Or, a wonderful tool for transporting possessed children without a fight.

I got behind her and looked over her shoulder. "Did you kill it?"

"Of course not," she snarled. "I simply found it here after everyone went crazy over graceless Gabe and his tumble."

"You did that," I said, sidling a bit closer.

"I did." She laughed.

When her head tipped back, I grabbed it and wedged my thumb at the very edge of her jaw, so she couldn't shut it all the way. I pushed the vial into her yawning mouth and dumped the liquid. In normal situations, I'd have dosed her juice or water. But sometimes quick decisions had to be made. Faltering could get you killed.

She bit the fuck out of me, but it was fine. The pain kept me alert.

When she sputtered, I reversed tactics and held her jaw, so her mouth stayed shut. I worked her throat. Hoping against hope I could get her to swallow reflexively.

Sometimes this part failed.

I felt her swallow despite not wanting to. Her throat worked convulsively.

But I kept her mouth clamped shut long enough for the liquid to dissipate no matter what she tried to do to avoid it.

When she slumped in my arms, I still held her tightly until I was utterly sure. History and experience had taught me how crafty these creatures could be. Especially the kids.

I let her fall into my embrace and then hustled her to my car parked at the very back of the parking lot. Always far back, in case I needed privacy or a covert getaway.

I dropped her in the trunk and duct taped her mouth. Then I tied her hands. So small and seemingly innocent. But strong enough to shove a kid down the steps. Or worse.

I returned to the church after locking my car. "Nothing," I said to Ellen, giving a defeated shrug. She turned away, back to the children, and I stood there watching. Waiting.

A little bit of time with the cops and then tapping out due to nerves and shock was the plan. Once off the premises, I'd take her home.

I THINK I'M ALONE NOW

My house has a bunker built by a paranoid man in the fifties. It's way back on my property. It's virtually soundproof. Forgotten by most people except for me. It's why I bought the house.

My home was about an hour from the church. No one knew where. I'd made sure of that. I would have to find another church if any suspicion was raised about me. I would have to find a new home.

I highly doubted that would happen. But I was always prepared for the worst.

The scar inside me kept me alert. The worry kept me moving. The fear kept me alive.

ACKNOWLEDGEMENTS

As always, I couldn't write any of my books without my family who allows my tangents, obsessions, and creativity.

My amazing husband who is my biggest cheerleader.

My daughter who asks the hard questions that make my brain hurt but make me a better writer with a better book.

My oldest son who roots for me even though I think he often forgets I'm a writer.

My youngest son who promised that if I did a book signing and no one showed up he'd buy all my books and make me sign them, each one.

And, of course, Grindhouse Press. This is my third book with them, and I couldn't be happier about it. Thanks for giving my bizarre and violent children a home.

Ali Seay lives in Baltimore with her husband and kids and the ghost of a geriatric wiener dog who once ruled the house. She's the author of *Go Down Hard* (Grindhouse Press), Hysteria: Lolly & Lady Vanity (Grindhouse Press), and *To Offer Her Pleasure* (Weirdpunk Books). Her work can be found in numerous horror and crime anthologies. When not writing, she hunts vintage goods, rifles through used bookstores, and is always down for a road trip. For more info visit aliseay.com

Other Grindhouse Press Titles

#666__*Satanic Summer* by Andersen Prunty
#101__*Cute Aggression* by Emily Lynn
#100__*Headless* by Scott Cole
#099__*The Killing Kind* by Bryan Smith
#098__*An Affinity for Formaldehyde* by Chloe Spencer
#097__*Kill the Hunter* by Bryan Smith
#096__*The Gauntlet* by Bryan Smith
#095__*Bad Movie Night* by Patrick Lacey
#094__*Hysteria: Lolly & Lady Vanity* by Ali Seay
#093__*The Prettiest Girl in the Grave* by Kristopher Triana
#092__*Dead End House* by Bryan Smith
#091__*Graffiti Tombs* by Matt Serafini
#090__*The Hands of Onan* by Chris DiLeo
#089__*Burning Down the Night* by Bryan Smith
#088__*Kill Hill Carnage* by Tim Meyer
#087__*Meat Photo* by Andersen Prunty and C.V. Hunt
#086__*Dreaditation* by Andersen Prunty
#085__*The Unseen II* by Bryan Smith
#084__*Waif* by Samantha Kolesnik
#083__*Racing with the Devil* by Bryan Smith
#082__*Bodies Wrapped in Plastic and Other Items of Interest* by Andersen
        Prunty
#081__*The Next Time You See Me I'll Probably Be Dead* by C.V. Hunt
#080__*The Unseen* by Bryan Smith
#079__*The Late Night Horror Show* by Bryan Smith
#078__*Birth of a Monster* by A.S. Coomer
#077__*Invitation to Death* by Bryan Smith
#076__*Paradise Club* by Tim Meyer
#075__*Mage of the Hellmouth* by John Wayne Comunale
#074__*The Rotting Within* by Matt Kurtz
#073__*Go Down Hard* by Ali Seay
#072__*Girl of Prey* by Pete Risley
#071__*Gone to See the River Man* by Kristopher Triana
#070__*Horrorama* edited by C.V. Hunt
#069__*Depraved 4* by Bryan Smith
#068__*Worst Laid Plans: An Anthology of Vacation Horror* edited by
        Samantha Kolesnik
#067__*Deathtripping: Collected Horror Stories* by Andersen Prunty

#066__*Depraved* by Bryan Smith
#065__*Crazytimes* by Scott Cole
#064__*Blood Relations* by Kristopher Triana
#063__*The Perfectly Fine House* by Stephen Kozeniewski and Wile E. Young
#062__*Savage Mountain* by John Quick
#061__*Cocksucker* by Lucas Milliron
#060__*Luciferin* by J. Peter W.
#059__*The Fucking Zombie Apocalypse* by Bryan Smith
#058__*True Crime* by Samantha Kolesnik
#057__*The Cycle* by John Wayne Comunale
#056__*A Voice So Soft* by Patrick Lacey
#055__*Merciless* by Bryan Smith
#054__*The Long Shadows of October* by Kristopher Triana
#053__*House of Blood* by Bryan Smith
#052__*The Freakshow* by Bryan Smith
#051__*Dirty Rotten Hippies and Other Stories* by Bryan Smith
#050__*Rites of Extinction* by Matt Serafini
#049__*Saint Sadist* by Lucas Mangum
#048__*Neon Dies at Dawn* by Andersen Prunty
#047__*Halloween Fiend* by C.V. Hunt
#046__*Limbs: A Love Story* by Tim Meyer
#045__*As Seen On T.V.* by John Wayne Comunale
#044__*Where Stars Won't Shine* by Patrick Lacey
#043__*Kinfolk* by Matt Kurtz
#042__*Kill For Satan!* by Bryan Smith
#041__*Dead Stripper Storage* by Bryan Smith
#040__*Triple Axe* by Scott Cole
#039__*Scummer* by John Wayne Comunale
#038__*Cockblock* by C.V. Hunt
#037__*Irrationalia* by Andersen Prunty
#036__*Full Brutal* by Kristopher Triana
#035__*Office Mutant* by Pete Risley
#034__*Death Pacts and Left-Hand Paths* by John Wayne Comunale
#033__*Home Is Where the Horror Is* by C.V. Hunt
#032__*This Town Needs A Monster* by Andersen Prunty
#031__*The Fetishists* by A.S. Coomer
#030__*Ritualistic Human Sacrifice* by C.V. Hunt
#029__*The Atrocity Vendor* by Nick Cato

#028__*Burn Down the House and Everyone In It* by Zachary T. Owen

#027__*Misery and Death and Everything Depressing* by C.V. Hunt

#026__*Naked Friends* by Justin Grimbol

#025__*Ghost Chant* by Gina Ranalli

#024__*Hearers of the Constant Hum* by William Pauley III

#023__*Hell's Waiting Room* by C.V. Hunt

#022__*Creep House: Horror Stories* by Andersen Prunty

#021__*Other People's Shit* by C.V. Hunt

#020__*The Party Lords* by Justin Grimbol

#019__*Sociopaths In Love* by Andersen Prunty

#018__*The Last Porno Theater* by Nick Cato

#017__*Zombieville* by C.V. Hunt

#016__*Samurai Vs. Robo-Dick* by Steve Lowe

#015__*The Warm Glow of Happy Homes* by Andersen Prunty

#014__*How To Kill Yourself* by C.V. Hunt

#013__*Bury the Children in the Yard: Horror Stories* by Andersen Prunty

#012__*Return to Devil Town (Vampires in Devil Town Book Three)* by Wayne Hixon

#011__*Pray You Die Alone: Horror Stories* by Andersen Prunty

#010__*King of the Perverts* by Steve Lowe

#009__*Sunruined: Horror Stories* by Andersen Prunty

#008__*Bright Black Moon (Vampires in Devil Town Book Two)* by Wayne Hixon

#007__*Hi I'm a Social Disease: Horror Stories* by Andersen Prunty

#006__*A Life On Fire* by Chris Bowsman

#005__*The Sorrow King* by Andersen Prunty

#004__*The Brothers Crunk* by William Pauley III

#003__*The Horribles* by Nathaniel Lambert

#002__*Vampires in Devil Town* by Wayne Hixon

#001__*House of Fallen Trees* by Gina Ranalli

#000__*Morning is Dead* by Andersen Prunty

Made in United States
Troutdale, OR
09/15/2024